Quite A Pleasant Little Journey

Peter Georgiadis

CIRCLE OF PENS
PUBLICATIONS LTD.

www.circleofpens.com

First Edition 2006 by
CIRCLE OF PENS PUBLICATIONS LTD.
www.circleofpens.com

ISBN 978-0-9552471-1-8
0-9552471-1-X

Cover and typeset by
Circle of Pens Publications Ltd. & Erik L. Lloyd

Printed and bound in Great Britain by
Cromwell Press Ltd., Trowbridge, Wiltshire

Acknowledgements

Many thanks to Wenche Georgiadis who worked tirelessly researching the historical facts for this book.

Many thanks to Brigitte Bonnet, without whom this book would never have been written.

Thank you also to David Bartlett, whose knowledge of the Great War is without equal and that is why he is the main character of this book. In real life he is a most decent, kind and gentle person.

Though this book is a work of fiction, the story is based on an historical event using actual names of individuals involved from that time. Most of the fictional characters are considered friends or heroes to the writer.

It has not been the author's intention to offend anyone.

I

David Bartlett was enjoying walking down Molesworth Road on the heights overlooking the reservoir, just outside the town of Plymouth in Cornwall. He had been on a daylong ramble, staying well clear of all other people by walking the country paths. He had satisfied himself with the knowledge that he was keeping his already healthy body in a prepared and always primed state for when he and his unit would be called for some sort of action.

The sun was just beginning to set, displaying a clear red-green-yellow haze over the sea; it had that appearance of a Turner painting, something completely surreal, almost abstract yet utterly beautiful. 'This is more like an impressionist painting than the real thing,' he thought to himself. He was completely captivated by this staggering panorama that revealed itself in all its glory before him. As the sunlight glistened in its dying moments, Lieutenant Bartlett just had to stop in his tracks and take stock of this day and its developments. Days like this, at this time, were precious: he knew just how close to hell Britain had fallen, so anything that distracted him from the reality of the situation was good news indeed.

He looked once more at *The Times* that he held in his hand and still could not believe the awful headlines that screamed at him. *'Eighty-three Thousand Missing in Action, Presumed Dead'*. He noted the date, 21st August 1917; these were the estimated dead from the first day of the battle up to the date of the article, and many more casualties were expected. Passchendaele was not giving up its ground easily: it had started raining the day the battle opened, and that precipitation was partly the reason for so many casualties. Soldiers were so overloaded that when walking to their jumping-off positions they might be unlucky enough to slip off the duckboards into shell holes filled with water; it was then up to each individual to extricate himself from the problems that had befallen him; many could not, and slipped further into the mire and drowned. It had taken more than a month for the truth to trickle through. What had at first been thought to be a victory had now shown itself to be yet another disaster, maybe the biggest to date, in this the Great War.

Lieutenant Bartlett was a tall thin man, now in his thirty-sixth year; he had constantly kept himself neatly dressed, his uniform always pressed as if ready for that snap inspection. He had slicked-down black hair, and sported a trim moustache in a pale imitation of the film star Douglas Fairbanks; this was the hero he had always craved to be. He even had what looked like a duelling scar over his left eye, but in fact it had occurred very prosaically when he fell off his bicycle as a small child. David had never married, mostly because he just didn't like women, whom he thought of as all being like his mother, rather boring; other than having babies and dealing with domestic work, they were superfluous to needs, at least in his life. He was not interested in men either, he just never thought about sex. It was something that other men bragged about, lusted after, but it left him feeling entirely indifferent. He never even masturbated; having tried it once, the excitement of the ejaculation was quickly overshadowed by the self-loathing caused by the resulting mess. Anyway, Bartlett believed that any form of discharge would only sap the strength that he demanded from his body.

He joined the Royal Marines at the beginning of the war in 1914, mainly to get away from the bank he worked for in Rye, Kent. There, he had worked his way up to Assistant Manager, but hated his position, hated the bank but most of all hated the Manager above him, whom he had always thought of as a complete and utter pompous fool, certainly not fit to manage a bank, even a small branch such as Rye.

Bartlett had had a very fine education. Lucky enough to attend the grammar school at Battle in Sussex – winning many prizes – he declined the chance to try for a degree in Commercial Studies at Birmingham University when, at the last moment, he was presented with an opening into banking. Encouraged by his aging parents, he saw this as a golden opportunity for regular work and a possible pension after retirement. He had cursed his missed chance from the first day of work.

David looked at the headlines again. He swore at the powers that be, then noticed that the sun was now making it hard to read, and at this he wiped some more blood from his right hand onto the newspaper, threw it into the hedge out of sight of prying eyes and thought how nice it would be to have a couple of drinks in the officers' mess prior to having an early night; with an untroubled mind he would sleep the sleep of an innocent child. At that he picked up his step and made his way back to the temporary barracks where he was billeted within the naval harbour area. His progress was slightly hindered by the encumbrance of the object strapped to his right leg, inside his trousers.

'Three bloody years in the Marines and not once have I been in any action. I need something to happen or I will go bonkers with frustration'. He quickened his pace even more as now it was becoming quite dark with just the last show of red sunset on the horizon. 'It will be another warm day tomorrow with precious little to do again, unlike those poor bastards in Flanders where it has not stopped raining since the battle opened on the 31st of July; please God give me some action, I need to flex my muscles, I need to feel all this training has not been for nothing, and I want my share of killing the Boche!' Looking up at the sky, he noted the whirling of skylarks, dipping and diving, as they hunted the myriad of insects that were airborne. He never failed to marvel at the grace of these delicate creatures and felt uplifted by their mere presence. Before he entered the barracks through the main gate, he once again checked himself to make sure that he was neatly turned out, slicked back his hair and walked through, saluting the guard as he did so.

3

Chief Inspector Harris, known to his few friends as 'Knocker' Harris, was the first to arrive at the spot where the local bobby was waiting with his whistle and his truncheon at the ready. He looked terrible to Harris, chalky white and shaking rather badly; he had obviously been quite sick some moments before.

They both stood on the edge of the wood some seven miles from Plymouth, going inland towards Milton Combe. This was an ancient area full of Roman and early Briton history; the woods had trees that went back hundreds if not a thousand years, and had seen kings come and go, wars fought, and many people murdered before, so nothing had changed as far as the trees were concerned, it was just normal human activity.

"What is your name, and who saw her first?" enquired Harris to the still shaking Police Constable.

"Sir, I am Constable Whitely, and I was called here by the local farmer, a mister…" he looked at his notes, finally putting his truncheon back in its sheath, now realising that nobody was about to jump out on him, "Mr. Martyn Jones of Black Pond Farm, which is just across the other side of this road." Colour was now starting to come back to his cheeks and his voice was definitely rising in confidence. "I, ah, allowed him to take his dog home and have a cup of tea as he was terribly shaken. He had been out hunting rabbits when he came across the body."

"Constable Williams!" Harris called, "Come here, lock the car door, and let's have a look together at whatever it is we have."

The three of them didn't have far to walk, not more than one hundred yards along a footpath, and there, just under an ancient oak tree was the body of a young woman, probably not more than twenty to twenty-five years of age. Harris stopped short, as did Williams and Whitely. The Chief Inspector felt the bile rise in his throat but somehow managed to prevent it from escaping; Williams was not so lucky. All three looked on in complete abject horror.

The young girl had been cut open from her navel to her chin, leaving most of her organs spread all over the ground. Blood was everywhere, and though she had obviously been slain at least twenty-four hours before, the blood around her sparkled in the sunlight that filtered through this venerable tree. Her eyes were wide open, and though her stare was that of a dead person, she nevertheless appeared as if terrified. There was nothing around her that showed any struggle, no broken bushes, not even crushed grass; it was as if she had stood there under the tree awaiting her fate.

"Bugger me!" exclaimed Williams, and promptly lost yet another meal. Chief Inspector Harris was still rocking on his heels when he realised that maybe a whole minute had passed and nobody had said anything. Both Williams and Whitely were now frozen to the spot that they stood on. Whitely started to pensively look around and once again began to nervously finger his truncheon. It was the Inspector that broke the spell, saying, "One thing for sure, this is too big for just us. Constable Whitely, go and make sure that Mr. Jones is in his house and stay with him; at this stage he is our only suspect. Williams, go back to a telephone and phone the station: we need help, this is going to take a team of specialists in murder!" The two Constables departed with great haste, leaving Harris at this place of great beauty and now wretched horror, all alone. He looked around without moving from the spot he was rooted to. After a moment or two Chief Inspector Harris sunk to his knees, placed his head in his hands and cried. He sobbed for all the sadness of this country, all the deaths, either by murder or accident, he wept for all the misery of the war, he cried for everything.

Chief Inspector Harris was a rather stout man of just fifty years, one who had had a few too many fine, and obviously too big, meals. He liked his wine and his beer, not that anyone had ever seen him drunk. In fact his colleagues liked him but had never really got to know him, as he was a rather private person. He was married with three sons, all past leaving-home age, but none had, preferring the life at home to making it out there in the big wide world. But the times had caught up with the Harris family, and the two oldest sons were now well and truly entrenched in the navy, both doing Channel patrols from Dover. The third son, James, liked his home comforts too much to think about following Michael and Andrew into the Royal Navy. While awaiting his call-up papers he was working in a small engineering company making components for aircraft.

Steven Harris considered his lot as being a happy contented existence. He felt the family had so far escaped lightly in the general bloodshed. Yet so many of his colleagues had lost loved ones through the ghastly mistakes daily being played out in the name of justice throughout the Western front that he knew every death was a waste of human life, and to what end? Nobody who thought deeply could see the sense of it any more. Coming across this tragic corpse had brought all these feelings to the surface in an explosion of grief.

He had joined the police force immediately after leaving school at the tender age of sixteen and worked his way to where he was now. Once again he looked at the body of the young woman, 'in all my years in the force I have never seen anything so barbaric as this.'

Less than one hour later there were twenty policemen of various ranks, searching through the undergrowth for any traces of weapons, or clues that might lead them to the apprehension of the perpetrator of the murder. The young woman had been so cleanly cut that there were no jagged edges to be seen on her skin or her clothing either. Chief Inspector Harris had now more or less relinquished his control of the case to another officer, in this instance an Inspector from the murder squad.

"My God, this is a grimy one!" said Inspector Cutler, looking over the unfortunate remains of the young lady. Cutler was a sturdy six-footer, who had spent fifteen years as a Sergeant in the Infantry, ending up by fighting in the Boer War. He had left the army after returning to Britain at the end of the South African campaign, having become totally disillusioned at the internment of the Boer women and children in concentration camps. After seeing so much death, joining the murder squad seemed like child's play compared to what he had experienced in the Transvaal.

"Steven, when you look at this cut, it must have been the sharpest instrument, to have cut through clothing, flesh and bone in one thrust. At least, it looks like *one* thrust."

"What amazes me is that there seems to have been no struggle; it was as if she was waiting for it to happen. There was no disturbance of undergrowth, not even trampled grass." Harris further added, "She does not have the look of a prostitute; there is something rather Sunday-schoolish about her. Surely someone will have reported her as missing, assuming she is local."

"Once we've cleared the area for weapons, I will get the doctor to examine the body for any sexual intercourse." At this, Cutler looked around for the first available Constable and ordered him to stand guard by the body. Turning back to Chief Inspector Harris, he quietly said, "I think it's time we interviewed Mr. Jones."

"So, Mr. Jones, I'm Chief Inspector Harris and this is Inspector Cutler. Do you mind if we come in?" asked Harris as he gently but firmly pushed his way through, looking for the parlour which happened to be the first room on the right. There was a low growl which took both the police officers by surprise; there, in the corner of the room, lying in a circular wicker basket, was the shaking, very nervous-looking black Labrador that was owned by the farmer.

"I had forgotten that you had a dog with you when you found the body. Is this the one?" enquired Harris. A nod of assent was farmer Jones' answer.

"Why is he shaking so badly?" asked Inspector Cutler.

"Wouldn't *you* be shaking? Like me, my dog's never seen a dead human before, in such a bloody awful way to boot. He may be only a dog, but he knows enough to knows that what happened out there ain't at all right."

"I suggest we all sit down, and talk this through. Firstly, what time did you leave the house to go shooting?"

"Me and the dog left just about five thirty this morning. We took the long route around the field over there," he said, pointing back across the road to the right of the woods, "we caught a few rabbits in the field, and I thought I might try my luck at some nice plump wood pigeons, er, that would have been by then about seven o'clock. We have a place which I will be happy to show you at the far end of the wood where there is a clearing, and if you throw some crumbs down, you might be lucky and attract the pigeons. We must have been hidden in the undergrowth for well over an hour, before I decided enough was enough. No birds for us today!"

"So what time was it when you got to the girl?"

"Well, I can only guess, but I reckon round about nine o'clock."

"What did you think when you saw her?"

"*Lawd!* What the hell do you think I thought? I was completely shook up! All I could think about was getting out of there and contacting you people, and for that I had to go all the way to Milton Combe where I bumped into P.C. Whitely, whom I've known for many years and I'm sure would vouch for me. When I'd told him what I found, I really don't think he believed me. But I showed him, and it fair took the wind out of both ourselves. He then contacted you."

"Our last questions for now, Mr. Jones. Have you ever seen the young lady before? Have you seen any other people around, and have you any idea who might have done it?"

"The answer to those three questions is real easy – no."

That night, back at the station, Harris, having looked at his watch, realising that he would once again be in the doghouse for missing his supper, turned to Inspector Cutler, saying "Fancy a drink, John?"

"Thanks, Knocker, have you got any whisky?"

"I never keep any here in the station. I don't want to be a bad influence on the rest of our force. No, I was thinking of a quick trip to the pub around the corner, the *Golden Cockerel*."

"Well, after our day, I think more than one is well in order!"

Both men leaned back in their armchairs, sipping their whisky and placing their feet on the fireguard. Though the fire was not alight, it gave a comforting feeling all the same.

"John, you have much more experience with murder than me, but there are two areas that I should point out, though I suspect that you are one jump ahead of me. I understand that we won't know for sure whether she was sexually assaulted for a couple of days, by which time I hope we will have discovered who she is. But there was something about her appearance that said maiden to me, not sexual. Firstly, what sort of weapon could have created such a devastating wound? From what I saw, I would have thought that it would have been an extremely sharp long knife, plunged in from the navel and pulled upwards. Just think how sharp that would have to be, and how strong the person was, to have taken it all the way up to the throat, cutting through bone as well. This brings me to suppose that there's probably remains, albeit fragments, of the blade inside her, something to look for, especially around the rib cage. Secondly, this has all the hallmarks of the Whitechapel murders by the infamous Jack the Ripper. So what I suggest is that you enquire as to any other similar murders around the country."

"I had thought of these things, but I'm happy that we both are thinking along the same lines. Two heads are certainly better than one. What about one for the road?"

The next day Chief Inspector Harris, arriving rather late for work, was informed by his duty Constable that a middle-aged couple, Mr. and Mrs. Richmond, had come to the station in a very fretful state, having read in the newspapers about the slaying of one young lady near to Milton Combe, as their own daughter, Cynthia, was missing. Harris looked at his duty clerk, and gave a long sigh of sadness, knowing this was the most unpleasant side of a policeman's job.

That morning, Lieutenant Bartlett rose as per normal at the sound of reveille, having spent a dreamless, refreshing night. After breakfast he went to see his Sergeant.

"Sergeant Laker, after you have drilled the men I wish that we could have a long hike as I feel they are becoming a little complacent, with not enough to do; anyway, after the fracas the other day, they can take this as punishment. It would be approximately a ten mile hike, with full kit, including rifles."

"Yes, sir. Does that include everybody, or do I leave out the men who already have prior duties?"

"No, Sergeant, the only ones who are excused have to be in front of a medical line-up. Is that understood?"

"Yes, sir. Ten o'clock all right, sir?"

"That will do nicely. Thank you, Sergeant."

At ten o'clock sharp, one hundred and twenty-eight subordinates, two Sergeants and six Corporals, all with heavy packs and rifles were standing at ease in the parade ground, awaiting the attention of Lieutenant Bartlett.

"Men, just a nice little jaunt into the countryside, where we will observe the birds and pick some wild flowers."

At this idle remark came a little titter of laughter from a section of the men, which gave rise to a smile from the Lieutenant, but a scowl from the Sergeants and Corporals. Sergeant Laker brought the men to attention, gave the order of quick march, followed hastily by left wheel, and then took position at the rear while Lieutenant David Bartlett led his men through the portals of the barracks onto the main road, the town proper on the way out of Plymouth and then the countryside. As they passed by the police station, Chief Inspector Harris took a moment to glance out of his window as he was disturbed by the sound of the marching feet. At first he thought that some sort of scare was going on, as it had been a long time since they had seen columns of soldiers going by, but as the men were obviously in uniform step, it quickly became apparent that it was just men playing at soldiers and he soon went back to the business at hand.

The lines of troops presently began to flag and started to spread out a little, which made the Corporals and Sergeants jump about bringing men into formation, playing catch up. Lieutenant Bartlett didn't give a tinker's cuss for what was going on behind him and was just striding out, enjoying yet another warm sunny day with a beautiful county ahead, where he could lose himself in sights and sounds. After only two hours and about six miles out, Bartlett, at the bequest of Sergeant Laker, decided to have a break; the Lieutenant would have carried on for hours had the Sergeant not run up to him in a rather sweaty panting state, saying that in his opinion the men needed a small breather. Most of the men were fine, but that could not be said for the N.C.Os who all looked just about done in. Bartlett smiled to himself with that knowing look on his face that showed Sergeant Laker he was fooling no one. But he was, if nothing, a thoughtful officer regarding his men, and after all, this walk or march, whatever he or anyone else thought of it, was really for his own benefit as it was a pleasure to have the company of his men. The N.C.Os and men actually were in admiration of their officer, whom they respected as being a very fair man, and Bartlett enjoyed being liked, so would unconsciously play up to the feelings of the men.

They had come to a small fishing hamlet called Newton Ferrers, which held within its small harbour about half a dozen crabbing smacks. There was a small church, big enough to receive twenty believers, an even smaller pub that also housed the store for food and all sorts of household requirements. Nobody seemed to be around, obviously having a siesta after their lunch. This surprised all the soldiers, because the sound of marching feet brings people from everywhere, but not there.

"Right, men, not more than half an hour's break, and the bar is most definitely out of bounds; I am not carrying anyone home, not unless they have a bullet in them, and I mean one from the Germans not the N.C.Os."

Again this brought a small ripple of laughter from the relaxing troop of men.

11

Bartlett walked over to the harbour wall, sat himself down, opened his rucksack and brought out a neat packet of sandwiches and a flask of water. He looked around to make sure that everyone else was resting and staying out of the bar; once he felt happy that all was well, he turned once again, gazing at the boats in the harbour and thought back thirty years to what he always tried to forget.

David Bartlett had been born to Margaret and Donald Bartlett in the year 1880, in the town of Bournemouth; he was very much a late comer as Margaret was already forty years old. She had given birth to a daughter eight years before David, and the rivalry for Margaret's love became apparent almost from the off. David's sister was called Helen, and she hated David, and used every opportunity to bully him and make his life a misery; as mum and dad were really more interested in a quiet life, they made sure they never noticed this problem between the siblings. David very quickly became withdrawn, taking every chance he had to be away from the house and Helen. But she would never leave it, and punching him became a way of life, except the punching became David's way of life too. But a boy could dream, and he did dream: he was going to be an explorer going into darkest Africa, he would follow his heroes across deserts and ice floes, he feared nothing, he had to be a hero; anything less would not be good enough. He had two other passions: one was to go bird watching; he knew all the different species, he could recognise what bird was what from very great distances. The second was to paint in watercolours, and of course it was nearly always his feathered friends that got their portraits hung upon his bedroom wall. He had very quickly become very proficient at his hobbies and family and friends were always impressed, except that is for Helen, who hated any kudos that David might attract.

It was on a Sunday charabanc trip from their then home in Guestling near Hastings, to Eastbourne that the tragic event took place. David, Helen and parents had decided to take a nice walk along the pier; the tide was high

12

and the water quite rough. Helen had been doing her normal impression of a loving sister, and whenever mum and dad were not looking would hammer a fist into David's arm muscle. This always hurt, but somehow David had become immune to the suffering, realising that Helen was just an evil person who was there on this earth to punish him for all his sins. He ran to the end of the pier, and there came across a set of steps going down towards the sea. This was a good place to find his hero status: why, he would swim to America from here, or at least to France. Helen, seeing him down there with no parents around, could not waste this precious moment. She followed him down some steps and started to torment him.

"Please, Helen, leave me alone."

"*Please, Helen, leave me alone*," she aped in grotesque response. "What are you going to do then, tell mum and dad?" She pulled a face at him then added, "You are just a mistake, a waste of space, no one likes you, and we all hate you. Why don't you die?" She then punched him harder than usual at which he recoiled back in pain. "If you don't stop, I will hit you back." Easy to say, but very hard to do. Helen swung her fist again at her younger brother, but this time he was prepared and just rushed her and pushed. Helen fell back hard, hitting her head on an iron handrail, then sunk down, sliding gently between the rails and dropping into the sea. She turned over onto her front with her face down in the water, then a wave just sucked her under and that was that. David looked at where she should be but nothing appeared; he rubbed his hands together, smiled, then thought, 'I should have done this a long time ago, it was very easy really!'

Mum and dad heard his explanation as to how Helen had slipped into the water, and how he had tried to pull her out, but she just disappeared. The police came, statements were taken and everybody thought that young David was a hero for trying to save his older sister. Her body was washed up onto the beach two hours later as the tide turned to go out again. The Bartlett family went into mourning, which gave David a chance to shine in his parents' eyes, and that for the first time.

Lieutenant David Bartlett blinked a couple of times, shook his head and looked at his watch. 'Time to get moving again.' He took one last lingering look at the sea, noting that it was as smooth as a mill pond; as he stared he became aware of gas bubbles seeping upwards to the surface from the seabed below in an eerie reminder of his sister's drowning. He sighed, called his N.C.Os together and got the men under way again. They took the long route back to the barracks, going inland via Plympton. They didn't go marching past the police station on the return, and anyway Chief Inspector Harris would not have seen the body of men, as just after the troops had gone past earlier, he had been called out to a small wood in Milton Combe; it seemed that a woman had been murdered, or at least that is what he had been told.

Bartlett and his men got back to the barracks just in time for a wash before eating a huge supper to restore tired limbs. It had been a fine couple of days, and for once David felt as if he had achieved something. 'Maybe things are about to turn for the better?'

II

Things had been going badly for the Allies in the war. A good example was the Battle of Loos in 1915 which was fought against the advice of General Haig. He considered it too risky for soldiers to mount a successful attack because of the way the Germans yet again held all the high ground; the battle had nevertheless gone ahead at the demand of General French, the then Commander-in-Chief of the BEF. The problems stemmed from the fact that the original plans had been drawn up by the French General Joffre who insisted that the British take the left side of the Artois region around the mining town of Loos, totally disregarding the magnitude of the German forces in that area as well as the difficulties presented by the terrain.

The Germans had a field day with the positioning of their machine guns and artillery, completely overlooking the Allies; the British Tommy was brave, bold and actually broke through to the small villages around Loos, but after a couple of days they were once again driven back to their original jumping-off positions; sadly the cost had been enormous, with thousands of casualties; Haig's prediction had proven true.

For this disaster General French was dismissed and General Haig took his place as Commander in the field. Unfortunately for Haig, he was thought of as an unimaginative leader, also rather dour, whose only concern seemed to be – 'If we lose one million men in battle, that's fine, as long as the Hun loses one million and one.'

The battle of the Somme which took place on 1st July 1916 was again introduced to the minds of the British by the French Commanders. Verdun was being besieged by the Germans who knew the French would never allow the enemy to take that area; this was of course just a battle of attrition to wear out the French army, killing as many as they could, hopefully forcing the French to come to the peace table. The trouble was that the battle for Verdun was also decimating the German army; who would be bled dry first? France needed a respite, and the way to obtain that was to start yet another battle elsewhere thus taking the pressure off Verdun.

So Haig was asked to take on the Somme offensive, which up until 1916 had been a quiet area within the Western Front. The British guns pounded the Hun line for twenty-four hours a day for eight days with more than three million shells; they thought that this would kill the foe and cut their wire; then at 7.30 a.m. huge mines were exploded under key sectors of the German lines and the battle had begun. The first problem that occurred was that the attacking troops were ordered to amble at a snail's pace across no-man's-land; why, they could even smoke their pipes should they so wish; after all, nothing would be alive on the other side!

How prophetic that statement turned out *not* to be! The shelling had not done its job; generally the wire was still intact, and the Germans were far from dead. Having had a couple of years of comparative peace in that sector, they had managed to turn their trenches into formidable fortresses with very deep bunkers for the front line soldiers to take refuge in, which they of course did. So when the bombardment and the mines stopped, they just came out of their dugouts with their machine guns, took careful aim at the walking, heavily laden Tommies, and then let rip with devastating fire. They had become good and mad at the British because of their continuous bombardment: it was surely time to make that contemptible little army pay, and pay dearly it did. Within one hour there were thousands of casualties; at the end of the first day there were more than fifty-eight thousand. Such heavy casualties made the public realise, maybe for the first time, that not only was the war going to drag on, but almost certainly, any battle was going to be hugely costly in terms of human life. If there had been a suitable replacement for Haig, the government would have certainly seized that option, but there was actually no one to take his place. This fact really stuck in the craw of the then Prime Minister Lloyd George, who couldn't stand General Haig.

It seemed to all, that Britain was hanging on by the skin of its teeth. Haig knew that to save his position as Commander he had to get a victory under his belt, and that was not looking at all easy.

The failures of 1916 had now turned into the failures of 1917. At least three thousand men were dying every day on one battle front or another; the manpower of Britain and its Empire was literally drying up. How much longer could this situation carry on for?

But gradually things were starting to improve. New techniques in warfare were being used: not just the creeping barrage but also gas attacks; it was not just the enemy that used the deadly gas. Once this had been used by the Germans in Ypres in 1915, the Allies were quick to follow suit, though at the time condemning the Germans as dastardly pirates and villains for using such terrible devices. The Allies soon mastered the techniques needed for using gas, and even evolved new types which included Mustard Gas, Chlorine Gas and a combination of many deadly chemicals, which became known as Yperite Gas, this being used by the French and British alike. Tanks were also being developed and used, at first with no real success, except maybe as scare tactics, but soon they would come into their own, being war's greatest development.

Then there was the war going on at sea. When war was declared in 1914, England had formed a formidable blockade against Germany, stopping the supply of raw materials and foodstuffs, thus preventing the manufacturing of arms and the feeding of the populace. This was to become a major factor in the ending of the war in 1918, as Germany began to starve. In return, the Germans had mastered the use of the U-boat, and throughout the war had successfully managed to sink more ships than Britain could build. But as always, the ying has a yang, and by sinking so many ships including unarmed passenger liners and neutral vessels, the Fatherland had become the pariah of the deep.

The sinking of the S.S. Lusitania, S.S. Sussex, hospital ships and many other ships of non-combative use had just gone to make the Germans look permanently like the aggressor, and as U.S. citizens were often among the drowned, this was fast becoming one of the straws that would break President Woodrow Wilson's back, thus eventually bringing America into the war on the side of the Allies. When the U.S.A. did finally declare war on the Central Powers, making available a further three million soldiers at least to come and if necessary, die on European soil, this provided a formidable and frightening number of extra fighting men for Germany to dwell upon.

But it was directly because the U-boats had become such a threat to Britain that the idea was born of blocking the ports of Ostend and Zeebrugge with obsolete large vessels, sinking them in mid channel, thus stopping the U-boats from having bases on the North Sea coast and the English Channel. At the same time an army could sweep up along the coast, taking the two towns and then pressing inland to push the Hun back to the Fatherland, and as the old joke goes, taking General Haig's drinks cabinet that much closer to Berlin. A plan was about to be born.

III

Chief Inspector Harris bent over his desk, stretching his arms and shoulders as he also yawned; he then looked at his cold cup of tea and wondered if it was worth getting Constable Martin to bring him a fresh cup. He decided it wasn't. Having now stretched his legs out as far as they would reach under the table, he crossed them. Leaning back hard on his Captain's chair he almost tipped it over, which would have been highly embarrassing as the room was full of subordinates awaiting some sign that there were things to do, concerning the Richmond case.

Inspector Cutler was the first to break the gloomy silence.

"The report, which I am sure you are all aware of, has come back from the boffins; it seems that Cynthia was completely unmolested, remaining a virgin, which considering her age, being twenty-six, seems quite amazing to me. They say that they don't think her underwear was touched at all except by her, maybe putting them on that morning. So we know that the killer was not killing for sexual pleasure, at least not any sexual sort of pleasure that I am knowing of."

He scowled at the assembled, as this last remark caused a little snigger. Cutler put his right hand index finger to his lips to yet again command attention, and then continued.

"So what do we have? Not much as yet, in fact precious little from what we already know, just a sexually uninterested maniac who enjoys killing. He has to have incredibly sharp weapons to hand, and if one thinks about it, they cannot have been big as he must have concealed them upon his person, since we have as yet found no trace of anything within the area.

And nobody has noticed any strangers or friends walking around with weapons bulging from their person... most peculiar; I can still only think that our man has destroyed or hidden very carefully both the dagger, for want of a better euphemism, and his clothing, which again I think must have been some sort of overalls as no one has reported seeing any blood-stained person ambling about; so where are these items? It has been over a month and really we still don't have much to go on. I know that most of you here have been doing your damnedest to find clues, but our boy has been clever, that is for sure. Now we also know that he must have been very strong to have thrust and pulled upwards so as to create the most damage in one go. What sort of man are we dealing with? I would suggest a tall man, as the angle of her body would indicate that the thrust was done whilst she was still standing up. Most of the spilt blood was falling down and not just across her person.

One thing we are waiting on is reports of any similar murders around the country; the trouble here is that the manpower within the constabularies is much reduced because of the war, but I am hopeful that we will get some answers to our enquiries in a short space of time now, from the rest of Britain's regions. Someone does not murder with such malice and then disappears, unless he knows exactly what he is doing, which also indicates that he probably has murdered before. So that also means our man is probably a travelling man, and what sort of men travel? Salesmen, engineers, businessmen or maybe just tramps, but surely none of us think that a tramp is what we are looking for, right?"

Chief Inspector Harris stood up and indicated that he wished to say something too.

"We have also thought of the armed forces as we have soldiers and sailors here by the bucketful. But on interviewing the Commander at the barracks just after the murder occurred, he said after consulting his records, that no soldiers had been allowed out that day, because there had been a fight on the parade ground, and as no one would talk about the incident, all the men had been confined to barracks for forty-eight hours; and the next day there had been a forced route march, which was supervised by a Lieutenant and Sergeants and Corporals, the only remaining soldiers being either on sick report or essential work detail. Though I know men can find ways of getting out of places and doing anything when they really want to, somehow in this instance I don't see it. Likewise, when I interviewed the Port Authority police, they assured me that as ships were actually leaving on patrol that day, there were very few men around that could not be accounted for. But that leaves dockers. They are strong, but they are generally not nomads by nature, and as work is plentiful, why would any stevedore be moving around? Of course they could, and we will keep punching away trying to find weaknesses. We seem to have drawn a blank so far.

Cynthia's parents are not sure if she was meeting anybody special; she didn't have a regular boyfriend, and they feel that if there had been someone in particular, then she would have told them. I asked them about her hobbies and interests, and was told that she was a huge reader of books, mainly novels, but when I asked if she read romances, the answer came back in the negative, which means to the less informed of you, no." Once more a small ripple of laughter pushed its way above the nominal silence.

"One thing they told me that might have a bearing, though, was that she was a great ornithologist, she loved her birds. But I was further assured that she would never go anywhere on her own. So if bird watching was what took her to the woods that day, it was an arranged rendezvous with someone she knew and trusted or thought she knew and trusted. But as mum and dad know of no such person, we are still drawing a blank. We must check out any groups of bird watchers, there must be a couple of organised groups in and around the area; maybe Cynthia had joined one of them? Anyway, Sergeant York, you start checking out that possibility.

As you know Cynthia lived and worked in Saltash; she was a typist for 'Morris, Morris & Clarkson', a reputable firm of solicitors. When I interviewed the head clerk, he also knew of no association between Cynthia, whom he had always known as a very private young lady, and any clients or local people. Once more a blank." Then in passing, as if no one else was in the room, he followed on with, "Oh, er, Martin, a nice hot cuppa for me and Inspector Cutler, please. The rest of you will be dismissed to do your duties very soon now, so there is no time for you to get a hot drink!"

This caused a huge sigh, and two smiles, one from Cutler, the other from himself.

"We don't have many more weeks on this case; I have been informed by the Chief Constable, a higher authority than me, that if no clues lead us to some sort of arrest within the next month, we will have to wind down the investigation, and that would be extremely sad, if not to say dangerous, as our boy will not end his fun until he is caught, tried and hung. I want you six," pointing to the six closest to him, "to go back out to the wood and this time prod and walk the ground of the local fields, see if anything shows itself to have been buried. The rest of you, back on the beat and keep asking those questions: *Seen anybody suspicious? Heard anything suspicious? Know anything suspicious?*" We need results and we need them now. Report anything you hear straight back to me or Inspector Cutler. Good hunting, now scram and work."

Turning back to his desk, Harris once again sat down heavily, yawned, leaned back and waited patiently until Constable Martin returned with two steaming cups of strong dark tea.

Harris sipped his tea, burnt his lower lip on the first attempt, nearly dropped the cup and growled at Martin as if all the world's problems were entirely down to him.

"I don't know, John, we have got nowhere with this case. It really bothers me that this maniac is still out there running loose. We must catch him."

Inspector Cutler looked sharply at his old friend, and then added, "I for one will not let this slip until the murderer is behind bars; if necessary I will keep on in my own time. We are of course missing things, but if we keep digging, something will turn up; you know it as well as me. Now I am going to make some of those telephone calls to different constabularies to hurry up replies to our request for information."

With that, he finished his piping hot tea in almost one slurp and hurried out of the main office into the eight-by-twelve foot cubbyhole which constituted the murder room.

Inspector Cutler finished eating and carefully folded the greaseproof paper that the sandwiches came in, as he was a man of meticulous routine that never wasted anything in life; his wife Ruth always made a combination of home cured ham and local cheese sandwiches on Thursdays which he enjoyed above all other days. It was at this moment that he remembered he was going to telephone the main constabulary in Edinburgh. He had spent all morning gradually working his way around the British Isles, using the major ports as focal points of reference. He had telephoned all the police stations that he had sent letters to, asking if there had been any similar murders, or deaths that did look suspicious. He knew it was important to follow up this way, as letters just get put aside and quickly forgotten. He hadn't got anywhere really, and had quite quickly become despondent, but that West Country *never say die* attitude kept him hard at it. He asked the duty officer in Edinburgh if they had received his letter which had been posted some time before; like all the letters sent, there had yet to be a single reply. He gave the reference numbers placed on all correspondence sent, and was asked to wait a minute while it was checked.

"Inspector Cutler?" chimed in a rather loud Scottish voice very suddenly out of the blue. Cutler jumped somewhat, as this did not follow the familiar pattern of negative answers: the new voice had surprised him to the extent that he nearly fell off his chair.

"Yes, I am Inspector Cutler, who do I have the pleasure of speaking to?"

"I am Sergeant Maclean. I understand you are the officer that sent out a special enquiry concerning strange deaths of women, is that right?"

"Yes it is, though I think I stated that it could also cover men as well. I have an unsolved murder here in Plymouth that just has that feel of a serial killer, and whoever committed this terrible deed must never be allowed to get away with it, so we here in Plymouth are spending more than usual time on the case. Do you have such a mysterious death that might in some way match?"

"Yes, sir, I do believe we do. A young woman was washed up on the beach near to Leigh, ah, about a year ago; in fact, to be precise it was on the 4th November 1916. It was thought that she had fallen off some sort of vessel and had her head sliced off; a few days later the head came ashore just a few hundred yards further up the coast. She was fully clothed, and had not been touched in any way, in fact she was still a virgin. Obviously, the head was more than a little battered by the force of the sea, but we estimated that she was between twenty and twenty-five years of age. We never discovered who she was, and no one has come forward to identify her remains. But you know, what made me and my chief really suspicious is that the head was cleanly cut off, as if in one slice. Now, if a propeller had done that, the mess would have been obvious to see. The coroner finally left it as an open case, but like you, we were short of manpower and have put the young lady on a back burner, er, so to speak."

"Sergeant, can you please send me down the reports that you have and maybe any photos too. I, in the meantime will talk to my Chief Inspector and maybe talk him into letting me come up and view all that you have more thoroughly. How does that sound?"

"Sounds fine to me, sir; I would, er, so to speak like to put this young lady to bed. Oh, that's not right. You know what I mean, sir, don't you?"

"Yes, Sergeant, I do. Many thanks; you are the only force to give me some sort of lead so far. Anyway I will be in touch again very soon. Thanks once again and goodbye... Oh, before you hang up, can you answer one last question? Is there, or has there been, a Royal Marines barracks nearby?"

"Yes, sir, I think so, but I will check it out and send the answer with the copied reports on our young lady. And good luck, sir, I look forward to hearing from you again. Is there anything else?"

"No, Sergeant, I will be in touch. Bye and thanks." Placing the receiver down once again Inspector John Cutler rubbed his hands together, smiled knowingly to himself thinking, 'maybe this is our breakthrough, I'll go and talk to Steven.'

"What do you think, Steven; can you swing it with the powers that be for the both of us to take a trip to Edinburgh? Why, we can make a little trip out of it; I am quite sure we would both appreciate a weekend away; think how refreshed we will be when we get back." He was almost pleading his cause to Chief Inspector Harris, showing his feelings with his hands in a state of prayer, up to his lips. Harris got up from his Captain's chair where he had been writing reports on various cases that the station was involved with; he strolled over to the window and looked out into the street. The first thing he noticed was that there was quite a bit of traffic going on in the town and many army lorries were coming and going from the barracks; he noted that their rate of speed was quite excessive for being in town. 'I bet those bloody drivers are doing fifteen or twenty miles per hour, far too fast for these bad roads.' He suddenly became conscious that the sun was starting to break through the clouds that had hung over the city like a wet blanket; the sun appeared to be finally winning the race, and long rays began to shoot down like arrows from the heavenly bow, getting stronger and appearing longer and longer with time. 'This is going to be ending up as a very warm nice sunny day. I should be out fishing.' Then with a jolt he remembered that his friend had been talking, and he came back to his senses.

"Scotland, ah! How long do you think we will need?"

"I would think not more than, say four days; with extra if we need it."

"Well, let us wait until all the papers appear, appraise what we see and take it from there. But in theory, and as it is our only lead, yes, I feel we should go."

The very next day when Inspector Cutler arrived at the station, he was greeted by a bundle of files, which contained the notes and photographs of the poor unfortunate woman who had been decapitated in Edinburgh. Cutler walked into his cramped little office with his newly acquired prize; but instead of proceeding at his normal slow yawning pace, as Cutler always seemed to be tired, he was surprisingly jaunty. Hanging up his jacket he sat down at his desk to open the bundle.

"Constable Riley, are you there?"

"Yes, sir, how can I help?"

"Two sugars, please, and make it strong; I have a feeling I shall need something powerful when I look at this little lot."

There were pictures with measurements of the victim at the beach, on a table in the morgue, from every angle with and without her clothing. Then pictures of her head, though not much could be recognised as it was very damaged from the buffeting that it had endured in the sea and from being washed ashore onto small rocks and shingle. Cutler thought how petite she seemed: her body was very firm with little breasts that had never suckled a baby, sticking quite erect. 'How desperately sad, this poor young lass has been born, got through childhood, made puberty, but never fulfilled her role as a mother as she was still innocent and virginal,' thought Cutler as he perused the grisly photographs. The tea arrived, and he had been right: he needed a strong cup. He read the reports of the Constable that had been the first on the scene, then the station report, and lastly the Coroner's. Wiping away water from his eyes, blaming the hot tea and not the reports, he decided it was time to meet with Steven "Knocker" Harris and see what he thought about the incident in Edinburgh, and whether he deemed there was enough similarity with their case for making the journey, or not? Had it been a boating accident or was it murder?

On entering Chief Inspector Harris's office, Cutler looked and saw his friend standing by the window, gazing out; he was surprised when the latter quietly said, "I do believe the Royal Marines are moving base. There has been major traffic from their barracks for the last couple of days, and now they seem to be removing some of their artillery." Harris sighed, and turned to look at his friend. "John, I guess that is the report from Edinburgh and not a copy of today's *The Times*; what do we have then?"

"I want your opinion on this one, Steven; I really do not know what to think. The only thing that makes me suppose that it might be murder is that it is such a clean cut, straight off, with no tearing, just like our Cynthia, clean and fast. But of course I might well be wrong, that is why I want a second opinion from you."

Harris scanned the photographs carefully; he quickly read the various reports, and all the time Inspector Cutler watched his friend with great interest. After what must have been an hour, with no interruptions of any sort from within the station, he stopped reading, scratched the side of his temple, placed the report that he'd been studying very carefully among the pile of papers that Cutler had brought for him to scan over. Cutler noticed that he had placed the last report with such reverence that one might have thought he was replacing the young lady's head upon her shoulders. Like Cutler, Harris was now quite white and looked more than a little shaken.

"So what do you think?"

"I am not at all sure either, but one thing I am sure of is that we should make that trip to Edinburgh together and see what we can find out believing that it is *not* an accident, but murder."

"You mean act as if we are already sure that she was slain?"

"Well of course, not much point in us going to confirm that it was just a nasty accident, is there?"

Cutler went back to his office, and this time he felt as if there was a spark materialising for the first time since poor Cynthia was killed in that savage manner. 'Maybe we will yet have someone's guts for garters,' thought Cutler as he started towards the telephone to arrange for the Inspector covering the case in Scotland, to meet them at the Waverley station when they decided to make the journey up there.

IV

It was another fortnight before both Chief Inspector Harris and Inspector Cutler were free from other cases and commitments, and able to make that train journey to Edinburgh. But their time had not been wasted, and both men had felt quite pleased with their clear up rate. Crime had been on the increase since the start of the war in 1914, especially as it was realised by the underworld that the police force were actually joining the army as well as everyone else, thus leaving all the constabularies around the country seriously undermanned. But there in the West Country city of Plymouth, with all that influx of sailors and soldiers, and all those various transient workers, the police were managing to keep on top of what had looked like becoming an impossible situation. Harris was proud of the way that his force was stoically keeping the lid on a potentially boiling cauldron.

It had finally been decided that they would travel on the 10th of October in that year of 1917. Tickets had been bought, and first class tickets at that; usually they would have been made to travel at best second class. But after all, this was a murder investigation and one didn't want intruders within their compartment: they might need to discuss the case. Anyway, that is the excuse that they had given to get the best seats on the train.

The day had finally come; it was still warm weather, almost hot, and the thought of taking overcoats was laughed at by both men. They had their suitcases packed, their papers stuffed carefully, if one can stuff something carefully, into briefcases: they were ready.

'This feels like a school holiday outing,' thought Harris, but kept that idea close to his chest. The truth was, that since the possibility of a journey to Edinburgh had been suggested, even though officially in the line of duty, the idea of having time away from Plymouth had made Harris become quite excited, and he was looking forward to those precious days away from the normal routine, and even home life. 'A change is as good as a rest,' he reminded himself.

Plymouth to London was an overnight journey, as the train didn't leave until nearly ten o'clock that evening, and would be stopping at all the major stations to drop and pick up the post. They decided to board the train at nine-thirty, and with thirty minutes to spare, pulled down the two beds that their compartment held, stowed their personal belongings and prepared themselves for a long night ahead. The old rust bucket was nearly empty, not that they would have been bothered either way. As the slow iron monster pulled out of the station, both men casually looked out of the window, smoked a cigarette and decided there was nothing to do but catch up on sleep. They soon fell into dream mode, and then with heads lying cosily on their respective pillows, they were soon lost in the land of Nod.

Once at Paddington station, they hailed a taxicab to St. Pancras, where a diverted express would transport them and around five hundred others, all the way to Waverley station in Edinburgh. The journey was long, taking around twelve hours, even though the only stops had been to pick up water and coal. This time the lumbering four-six-two train was full of soldiers and sailors, but they were all busy doing whatever soldiers and sailors did on trains and were of no trouble to the policemen. Fortunately for the two men, there was a restaurant car on board, so both had felt well catered for. But soon the journey became a long drawn-out bore. Though the countryside was new to both of them, it soon became uninteresting, being flat along the east side of England, too industrialised, with grey towns and poor looking arable land. To them even the cattle and sheep looked colourless and sad; they were already missing those pretty downs and tors that Devon and Cornwall are so rightly proud of. They soon lost interest in viewing out of the windows, and just fell into a sort of stupor, brought on by complete and utter boredom. They arrived at Waverley at nine forty-five that night. Even though they had had nothing to do but read, talk and sleep, both of them felt completely exhausted, and were extremely glad to see Inspector McFry waiting for them, to take them to their hotel, maybe have a quick drink and make arrangements for the next morning. That night in their rooms in Hotel Constance, they quickly fell into the sleep of the innocent, out for the count, dead to the world. They were woken at seven the next morning with the local paper and a cup of strong tea. They washed, shaved, breakfasted and met McFry in the lobby of the hotel, who then drove them to the main police station. Now they were ready for what Edinburgh and murder had to throw at them.

"Good morning, gentlemen, I am Chief Inspector Turner, but please call me Alan. May I be the first to welcome you formally to Edinburgh, and let me assure you that we here at the station will assist you in any way that we can. Everything will be open for you, and wherever you wish to go and visit, transport and personnel will be made available."

"Well, Alan, that is extremely kind of you. I am Chief Inspector Steven Harris and my colleague is Inspector John Cutler, and we are both happy to be here and meet you and your colleagues. We have no preconceived ideas of what we want to do, except visit the site on the beach where your lady was first found. By the way, have you any name for her yet?"

"We still do not have any idea who she is; no one has come forward in this last year, so we have named her Lady Jane."

"And is Lady Jane still in the morgue or is she underground?"

"She was interred more than…" he looked towards his duty officer for some moral help.

"Er, about three months ago, sir," came the information from Constable Lawrence.

"About three months ago," answered Alan Turner as if no one had heard the Constable. "Anyway, would you like a cup of tea before we get seriously involved with whatever you decide you want to do?"

Harris looked at Cutler, then turned back to Chief Inspector Turner. "You are very generous to us, for which we are truly grateful, but if you don't mind, Alan, we will pass on the tea for now; maybe we can go direct to the beach just to get a feel of the place, if that is alright with you of course."

"Not a problem. Inspector McFry has been assigned to you for as long as you need him; he has the use of a car and driver, so you shouldn't have any problems finding your way around."

They all shook hands, then Chief Inspector Turner pivoted on his heels and made his way back into his office, leaving the two visitors and McFry to find their way to the beach at Leigh. They passed through the suburbs of a very grimy city; both the West Country policemen were so far very disappointed with what they had seen outside of Cornwall: everything seemed so grey or black to them, with dirty buildings and too much smoke; and even more, the people seemed ashen and tired; their first impressions were decidedly not good ones. When they reached the shore at Leigh, the water was very dirty: full of oil slicks, mud instead of sand, and flotsam and jetsam everywhere. There was so much floating along the shore they soon realised why Lady Jane's head was in such a poor state. They were shown the area where the body had been washed up; the first thing they noticed was a dead dog, floating, bloated and rotting on the shore line. They were then shown further along the beach where the head had turned up; this area was full of shingle and rocks, again demonstrating how easily the head had become damaged. Both men felt very depressed at the appearance of the shoreline: this was not the sort of beach that they knew in Cornwall.

"One question I asked your duty Sergeant when I first made contact was, were there any Royal Marine barracks in the area, but I never heard back from him."

"We will have to ask the Sergeant that when we get back to the station. For the life of me, I don't know what army, navy or any other forces are here in Edinburgh. As the poor Lady Jane case was quickly wound down, very little investigation took place. But if you asked Sergeant Maclean for information, he will have got it for you. If you have seen enough, we will make our way back."

Harris looked at Cutler to seek confirmation and turned back to Fry.

"Yes, time to get back."

It was lunch time when they reached the police station again, and much to the surprise of both Harris and Cutler, the station had its own canteen with real hot food, cooked on the premises. Harris and Cutler had never heard of, let alone seen, such extravagance as a canteen, in any other constabulary anywhere else before.

'Wow,' thought Cutler, 'now *this* is living, and so cheap.'

Both men indulged themselves fully with chicken soup, sausage and mash, with oodles of gravy, then completed with steamed suet pudding and custard.

"I tell you what, John; I might get myself transferred to this station if this is the norm."

"Behind me, I was two jumps ahead of you there."

After that satisfying lunch, they met up with Sergeant Maclean who turned out to be a huge mountain of a man, standing six foot eight inches high, weighing in at least twenty stone of pure muscle and fibre, with not an ounce of fat to be seen, and sporting a broken nose and looking as if he could squeeze sap out of a cricket bat. Both Knocker and John looked at this giant in wondrous awe.

"It is a pleasure to meet you both," said Maclean in the broadest of Scottish accents, so broad in fact that both the West Country police thought it was a foreign language at first.

"The pleasure is all ours," answered Harris, reluctant to give his hand to shake in case it was irreparably damaged, but actually finding the titan to be an extremely gentle giant, not quite what they were expecting.

"So did you both have good journeys up here?" he asked, this time shaking Cutler's hand.

"Long and boring, but we are both happy to be here and we really hope that this can be a mutually beneficial trip for all of us." John then added, "Did you give any thought to our question concerning the Royal Marines, or any other group of soldiers, sailors, in fact anyone that might have trickled down from your Edinburgh to our Plymouth?"

"I did, sir; indeed if you hadn't come up to us I was going to telephone you with what I discovered. In fact at the time of Lady Jane's unlucky experience," at this silly remark he smiled knowingly, and then continued, "I enquired as to what army groups were in the immediate area, or indeed as far away as Glasgow. But I didn't have to go that far, just outside the City, in the area of countryside just beyond the town of Musselburgh, not more than eight or nine miles from us here. There the Royal Marines had a training camp, very hush-hush, no one would talk about it, and when I tried to make enquiries I was very quickly warned off. Told in fact, to mind my own business, and not to make waves; nothing was more important than winning the war, so if I kept asking questions with anything concerning the Royal Marines, it might well mean that I was breaking into the official secrets, and so on."

At this point he stopped to gather his thoughts, took a large breath of oxygen to expand his lungs, and then carried on. "When I told them that it was a possible murder enquiry, still I got that negative answer. No one would talk about them. The only breakthrough that I got was when I went around the corner from where the barracks were situated, and asked about them in the local pub, the, erm… *'Weavers' Arms'* I think it was; I managed to speak to the landlord, and he admitted that the soldiers there often used his pub; in fact he went as far as to say that there were many fights, among themselves and the local population; but if that was the case, then nothing was ever reported back to us. But here is the interesting bit: they left their barracks there in Musselburgh just about ten days after Lady Jane's body was washed ashore. The landlord thought that they had either got overseas posting, or had moved down to Harwich. How about that, is it any help?"

"Help," said the amazed Harris with his mouth almost touching his chest, "if you worked for me, why I would have sacked the Inspector here and given you his job!"

They all smiled at this last remark.

"This is something very positive to work on. We have had no luck with our investigations whatsoever, but now I really start to think that the Royal Marines, or at least one of them, is going to have a lot to answer for. When I approached them in Plymouth, I had no trouble getting through to the Commanding Officer, but he was quite uncooperative regarding our line of questioning, claiming that on the day of the murder all his men were confined to barracks. But maybe he is not telling us all he knows? I don't care to hear excuses concerning a war: if someone murders in such brutal ways, then they must pay with the hangman's noose." With this, Harris clenched his fist, ground his teeth together, squinted and nearly burst a blood vessel, as the pent-up rage started to take control of his being. He made himself calm down; not that the other two had noticed, but he knew he must not strain his heart too much, as he had had warning signs some time back, yet had managed to keep his personal health worries away from his work. Being just eight years away from retirement and a well earned pension, he didn't want to spoil his chances of getting a reasonable work-free period of rest, and with money to spend.

"Steven, maybe we can use the telephone to see if anyone in Harwich knows of the Marines being encamped around the area. It must be worth the trouble, especially as there would be no way we can find out if they have overseas postings? If they have been there, then let us leave Edinburgh and go there. We can do our own impression of Sherlock Holmes and Doctor Watson, and guess who is going to be Holmes? Why, we can use our time and see what we can dig up."

'Harwich, where's Harwich?' wondered Harris as he followed Cutler and Maclean to the telephones.

"Operator, this is Inspector Cutler of the Serious Crime Squad within the Devon and Cornwall constabularies; can you get me a number for the main police station in Harwich? Yes, I did say Harwich, which I believe is a port town along the lower eastern reaches of England."

He sighed and shook his head in astonishment that the girl was obviously so ignorant.

"What do you mean by saying Edinburgh is a long way from Cornwall, don't you think I am aware of that? Do I have to tell you what I am doing in Scotland before I can get the number I want? Yes, the police chief knows I am using the telephone. Crikey, just get me the number; I don't want the third degree. What, you don't understand what a third degree is? Give me strength!" At this he handed the telephone receiver to Sergeant Maclean. "Please, help me out here."

"Girl, just get the number the Inspector wants, and don't be rude, or you will be looking for a job elsewhere; in fact I will make it my personal assignment to get you transferred to Harwich, and believe me, you won't like it there." He winked at the others in that knowing way, with a half-smile upon his face. Less than a minute later the telephone was handed back to John Cutler with the ring tone of the main police station buzzing in his ear.

"Hello, duty officer speaking. Can I help?"

"Hello, I am Inspector Cutler, from the Plymouth constabulary; at this moment I and my chief are in Edinburgh. We are here to follow up on a lead, which I am now hoping that someone there in your neck of the woods, so to speak, will be able to help me with. We have had an awful murder in Plymouth of a young woman, who has been cut from her midriff to her chin. We have also found out that a young lady in Edinburgh has been decapitated, and there is something familiar that draws us to believe we are looking at the same culprit. Our investigation so far has drawn very little in the way of clues, but we have established one vital clue, and that is that a section of the Royal Marines was around within the area. But before they came to Plymouth, having left Scotland, we are wondering if they came to Harwich? And that is where you obviously come in. Do you or any one of your colleagues know if they did encamp within the Harwich area? Sorry, we are talking just about a year ago or at least eight months."

"Yes, sir; there were reports, albeit more chatter than fact, that there was an encampment not far from the docks; we think they were here for some sort of training, but you know as well as I, anything to do with military is very much no go areas."

"Who am I speaking to?" Cutler followed with, before the receiving police officer could carry on.

"I am Constable Border, sir. On thinking about your request, we too had a mysterious death of a young woman. She had died from extremely deep cuts to her upper torso, very unpleasant. Her name was Wendy Bryant; her father is a councillor here in Harwich, and we too have had no luck with our investigation."

"Right, Constable Border, can you book two rooms in the local hotel for one Chief Inspector Harris, and me, Inspector Cutler. We are coming down tomorrow, and will come direct to your station. Can you please also arrange that we have the officer in charge of that case present and able to give us the time we need when there?"

"I can see no problem with that, sir, just call us when you know the time of arrival and I or someone will be at the station to meet you. This is all quite exciting. Have a safe journey. In the meantime I will talk with the chief and get permissions that might be needed. Is there anything else?"

"No, Constable, you have been very helpful and we look forward to meeting you tomorrow, sometime. Bye and thanks." Replacing the receiver, with a wide grin stretching from ear to ear, he looked at his friend and continued: "Wow, Steven, by gum I think we are onto things."

"Well, I suggest that we spend the rest of the day doing a bit of sightseeing, are you up for that? I will just go and give my thanks to Chief Inspector Turner and all that have helped us here."

Turner and several other officers who had been curious about the case appeared as if by magic to say goodbye to their two guests from the far Southwest. It had been a brief interlude, but one that all concerned felt to have been valuable.

"Chief Inspector, you have shown us real courtesy and we are both very grateful. I feel that with what we have learned here and hopefully in Harwich, we will nail the swine that has perpetrated these hideous crimes. He must be a madman; no one in any sort of right mind will contemplate such appalling ways to kill young ladies. But mad or not, I want to be there when they place that noose around his neck. We will of course keep you up to date with the on-going investigation."

V

Their train down to Harwich was yet again a slow lumbering old 060 that was more used to pulling coal wagons than a human cargo; there were no toilets, and no buffet of any sort, and by the time they reached Colchester to transfer to the Harwich train it was already late in the afternoon. Hunger was upon them in a very acute way, stomachs rumbled and mouths salivated, yet even at Colchester, a mainline station, the buffet was closed, *'As there is a war on, closed until further notice.'* They could not believe their misfortune, and stomachs, like the trains, just kept rumbling on. The train to Harwich was just two carriages long and filled to overflowing with people, so much so that the two policemen had to stand the entire way. They were hungry, thirsty and extremely tired. But as promised, there, was Constable Border who first took them to their hotel, then on the insistence of Harris, agreed to join them for a meal. The poor Constable could not believe his eyes when he saw what the two Inspectors tucked into. Oxtail soup, followed by steak and kidney pie with all the trimmings that the restaurant could muster, ending up with rice pudding, then more rice pudding. When they finally washed the whole meal down with a pot of strong tea and lit cigarettes, they sat back and surveyed their new surroundings.

"God, it is flat around this area!" said Cutler to no one in particular. "Is there much going on here, Constable Border?"

"Please, sir, we are off duty, call me Eric." Then he added, "Yes, we have our fair share of criminals and crime, mainly foreign sailors trying it on. But there are also hardened scum that prey off these sailors, and the amount of murders is quite awful; many sailors are washed up on the beach, or found with their throats cut in some dark area of town. The sad case of Wendy Bryant is a case in hand: she had a book, very beautifully drawn, on bird life lying close by her and we think she was probably killed for sex, but maybe the killer was scared off by someone else being in the area. Nothing was stolen, so we don't think it was a local thug, and her clothing was untouched, as was she. She was still a virgin, completely intact, if you know what I mean?" He then added, not waiting to be asked, "Her parents are in a terrible condition: her father nearly died after suffering a heart attack, and her mother hasn't spoken since the act occurred. I want to see the scum that did this hang, as I guess you both do."

Having now rested and fed, the Inspectors decided on a stroll around the harbour area.

"Will you join us for a little walk, Eric?"

"Not unless you wish to continue the conversation concerning Wendy Bryant; I have a wife and four small children to go home to." He smiled at the West Country police, but their mind and eyes were elsewhere.

"Will you be available to show us around tomorrow, Eric?" enquired Harris. He had taken a strong and immediate liking to this young Constable, who obviously showed that he didn't suffer fools gladly, and hoped that he would be the one to be made available for them both that next morning

"Yes, sir, I am certain that it will be me, if that is all right with you two, that is?"

"Then, Constable Border, Eric to his new friends, go home to your family and come and pick us up, say," looking at Cutler for support, "say ten o'clock in the morning, which gives us time to rest and refresh ourselves. Agreed?"

"Agreed, and thank you, sir; I look forward to working with you both." Once again he smiled an unseen smile, turned on his heels and drove the car back to the station, picked up his pedal bike and departed for home.

"John, come on, let's walk down to the quay."

They walked the hundred yards or so to the water front, turned right to walk along as far as they could until the barriers in the road and pathways halted them from going any further; everything was dark and dreary: the only street lamp shone directly to the ground and showed any passer-by that there was a gas lamp there, nothing else. The whole atmosphere was somewhat depressing; for a shipping port it was surprisingly quiet. Their footsteps echoed upon the cobbled roadway, and as they clonked their way along, they became aware of a sea mist which was starting to swirl and make its presence known, but over there in the distance was a clear area which could be seen, and the two men made for the best position to see out onto the water. Stopping and looking out into the estuary of the river Stour, they were very aware of the massive amount of shipping that was unloading or loading their cargo; and yet, though there was all this activity, it was surprisingly quiet: the dockers, lighter men and all the humans that were involved with the disgorging of freight from the bowels of the ships must have had it down to a fine art, as you could fall asleep to the rhythm of the noise, but yet somehow find it far from disturbing; such were the thoughts going through the brain of Chief Inspector Harris.

"I have been thinking there has been a connection that has been staring right at us all the time, yet so far we haven't taken a great deal of notice concerning it. The connection between the women has been ornithology, bird watching! The parents of Cynthia said in their statement regarding their daughter's hobbies how interested in watching and drawing bird life she was. Obviously, until we get to know who Lady Jane is, we will not find out if there is that connection there, but I would hazard a guess that there is; they could have been watching sea birds at the time of the murder. I realise it is all a little vague, but what else have we to go on?"

"Steven, you are right; I had thought that the birds might have something to connect the girls with these murders, but tiredness has kept me from seriously analysing all the information that has been collecting within our brains. Why, PC Border told us how the only thing they found next to the body of… what's her name? Wendy something or other, was a book of bird drawings. Sorry, Chief, but my brain has finally exploded, and if I don't get some sleep, so will the rest of me. Let's carry this on over breakfast."

The two men turned and walked back the way they had come, only to be stopped by a police Constable on night patrol, who wanted to know who they were and what they were doing in a restricted area near the docks at this time of night. "After all, had they not noticed the barriers?"

Back at their hotel they both crept to their respective rooms and slumped into the rather sagging metal-framed beds, which, though very uncomfortable, didn't stop two tired bodies sinking into dreamless sleep.

The next morning the two police officers appeared at the dining room to be greeted by the waiter, and informed that breakfast had finished at eight o'clock, and as it was now nine o'clock, well, what could he do?

"For one thing, get us two boiled eggs each, lots of bread and jam, and make that brew good and strong. Erm, one other thing, you had better be quick or I will see to it that your feet don't touch the ground on your way out!"

The startled waiter stood to attention as if someone had stuck a red hot poker up his rear end, turned on his heels, and almost ran out towards the kitchen. Though he was mumbling many things under his breath, the only thing the policemen heard was: "Well, I really don't know…"

Despite their little domestic upset, breakfast was as quick as it was abundant, and they enjoyed the food and tea very much.

"Now I feel like a new man," said Cutler, rubbing his now contented stomach.

"What is the time, John, and what time is Constable Border coming for us?"

"Ten minutes to ten, and my guess is that he's probably waiting outside right now; if not I'll pay for breakfast."

"You are on, let's look and see." Leaving a couple of coins for the waiter, which was only going to confuse him more, they made their way outside, and sure enough, there was Constable Border polishing the front window of his Austin police car.

"Bugger, did you have a sneak look?" enquired Harris to his friend.

"Would I cheat? The very idea!" But a wry smile appeared on the refreshed face of Inspector Cutler.

"Good morning, sirs, I trust you both slept well?"

"Good morning, Constable, yep, we both slept sufficiently, thank you. Now, first I think we should go direct to your station and let your chief know what we are about. Then we will ask you to take us to the victim's place of murder. After that, we will play it by ear, if that's alright with you?"

The station was a huge rambling early Victorian building that was once used as a cottage hospital for sailors who had been offloaded from their ships, having exhibited symptoms of some mysterious alien disease; in fact it was an isolation hospital. But there had been precious few patients over the last seventy years, and now it was easier for ships to unload their human cargo within the river Thames going up to London, as there was also another such hospital near Dartford but right onto the river. So Harwich's special needs hospital having no more special needs had become the town's main police station.

Chief Inspector Harrington was there to greet the strangers from the Western regions. He was a bearded, stout and neatly turned out man in his early sixties, just playing out his remaining years in the force, waiting for that elusive gold watch, and a small but very welcome pension. He had plans to buy a small cottage in the county of Lincolnshire, where both Ethel his wife and himself could potter and grow flowers and vegetables, and maybe rear a few chickens and rabbits to supplement their diet. They loved the idea of being self-sufficient, eating the good things that God supplied, having given them the power to grow the produce themselves. Charles Harrington and his wife were very forthright Methodists, and the way the World, Europe, England and Harwich were going, they wanted nothing more to do with any of it. As far as they were concerned this state of affairs was the twentieth century's Sodom and Gomorrah, no place for decent people.

"Good morning, gentlemen; hopefully you are refreshed from your night's sleep and ready to take the fight against criminals on board once again?"

A large grin appeared on John Cutler's face, but disappeared quickly when he realised that the Chief was serious in his remarks.

"It is a pleasure to meet you, sir," he said "and thank you for all your assistance. I hope that both of us can help solve the murders that have been going on around the Country. Thank you also for making a car and driver available to us, very much obliged to you." He held out his hand to shake Harrington's. "This is Chief Inspector Harris; sorry, sir," he said looking towards his friend, "I should have done the introductions first."

Harris held out his hand, only to experience a rather feeble grasp from Harrington, not what he expected.

"Please, tell me, how can a Chief Inspector and an Inspector both work on the same case? Don't they need you back in Plymouth for other duties?" Harrington was looking directly into the eyes of Harris, which made the later turn quite red with embarrassment.

"I, too, feel very strongly about this specific case, it was a particularly nasty killing. We, Inspector Cutler and I, are adamant that the perpetrator should feel the rough coarse rope of the hangman. Anyway, I had some time coming to me and I thought we could help one another on this case. Really I am working for Inspector Cutler and not the other way around."

"We now know that with your lady, one Wendy Bryant, it's looking likely that three victims have been slaughtered, and I do mean slaughtered, not killed, but hacked in the vilest way possible, and for what reason? We believe that they have been killed just for the sport of killing. None of them have been touched in any sexual manner; they were virgins to their deaths. But we now have several leads. First, it would seem that at least two of the ladies were ornithologists. Second, we have tracked it down to the possibility of a member of the Royal Marines being involved, as around each crime location there has been a Marines camp. What we have not established at this point is whether the Marines are from the same unit, and if so, who is the bird watcher? Then we have our man!"

Inspector Cutler breathed in deeply and let his eyes watch the reaction on Harrington face. None was forthcoming; he was as impassive as the moment they had met. After all, what is another murder more or less? This was the time for murder whether here in England or in Flanders fields; murder was rife and getting worse, this had become the way that Harrington thought. A Constable entered the office bearing three cups of tea. No one had asked for it, no one even asked if milk and sugar were needed, both were added anyway; only Constable Border stood, having not been offered a chair, and watched his superiors sipping at the dark brown liquid.

"So what are your plans today, then?" enquired Harrington.

"I thought our first port of call should be where the poor luckless lass met her death. Then we wish to go and see what is known about the Marine camp, who they were, how long they stayed and where they went next?"

John then looked at Steven to see if he wished to add anything else; nothing was said.

"Well, gentlemen, I wish you every success and God be with you on your quest for the truth. I really thought that the rascal that killed our Wendy was going to be a foreign sailor who would have long since left these shores, and would never be seen again. But I will be happy to be wrong, and extremely elated to hear that another evil devil has been rightly sent down to hell."

The two Inspectors and Constable Border left the station and climbed into the car supplied. Harris looked at Cutler and didn't know whether to laugh or cry: Harrington was not their sort of Chief Inspector; not understanding him or his way of life, they considered him a rather stupid caricature of a man, more suited to working as a minister of the church than running a busy police station. They did not know of his incredible early life in the force, personally bringing many serious offenders to justice. He was and still was, highly respected within the station and in the area. He had just grown old and worn out, disappointed with what life and times had thrown at him, that was all.

They drove six miles west of where they had been in Harwich, into where part of the river Stour can flood onto the plains: a very swampy area which of course was ideal for bird watching, it was midway between two villages, New Mistley and Bradfield. These two sleepy little hamlets had never experienced anything as terrible as the slaying of young Wendy Bryant before, and people were still in a state of shock. Constable Border told his two new colleagues how upset the folks were when the body had been discovered, and how people were always looking over their shoulders expecting something equally as appalling to happen again. Fingers were pointing, tongues wagging; this had caused several fights between men from each village, and one poor fellow had had his finger broken in a scuffle when he couldn't tell his accusers where he had been on the night of the murder. It seemed that everyone had become a Sherlock Holmes.

Border said, smiling to himself, "Maybe you are the only two who can bring peace back to this place?"

"Well, let's hope so, though I do not think anyone from these little places need fear being accused; I am reasonably sure we know where our man is hiding, it is just a matter of flushing him out." John Cutler looked at Constable Border, and then followed up this statement with, "Eric, I could use a favour from you; after we have left here and you go back to the station, can you, or can you get someone else to look up the names and addresses of Bird Watching groups within the area? Ask Wendy's parents what society she belonged to, if any. Now we have this connection we must pursue the line with vigour. When we know the organisation Wendy attended, we can find out if they had a Royal Marine as a member, then Bob's your uncle and Fanny's your aunt, we will almost certainly have our man. Can we now see the actual ground that the murder took place on?"

They scrambled down a small track that led near to the river; it dropped around eighty feet in height and was well out of the way of people and houses. Around them was dense undergrowth, mainly bramble and beach bushes, with many stinging nettles and dock leaf. Then about fifty yards from the now receded tide was the clearing. The spot where Wendy was killed was just behind some natural cover; no one could possibly see them, but they could watch all that was going on around them, an ideal location for ornithologists going about their business of watching birds. The three police officers stood, taking in the whole ambience of the site.

Harris broke the spell first. "I think we should go and find that Marine camp now; we have seen and done all we can here. The entire place has already been combed clean by you lot." Then looking at Border, he added, "Did you find anything else, other than the book of birds?"

"No, sir, not a thing; whoever did this didn't even leave much blood around. And nobody at all saw anyone suspicious at that time. All very strange. But I do understand where our Chief was coming from when he closed the case, believing it to be a foreign sailor who would have already sailed long into the sunset. We have many terrible crimes within the port area, and more often than not, if they come to court it was a foreign sailor, drunk or lustful."

They made their way back to the car, only to find two little boys playing around and banging into it. Being a gentle soul, Constable Border just glanced a slap around the top of one of the lads, who in turn jumped back, then turned with his eyes watering, ran across the street, looked back and said… "I'll tell my mum about you!" He then pulled his tongue out and ran off, with his mate close behind.

Once in the car, Harris asked Border, "Do you think you know where the camp might have been?"

"I have an idea, but it might be difficult to get any real information about them or where they stayed, or what they did when they were here.

I guess the best way around this problem is to go to the normal Territorial Army barracks, and quiz them there; what do you think?"

"I think," said John Cutler, "we are entirely in your hands, and your ideas are as good as anything; you know the area, we have never been here before." 'And won't come again when we leave!' were both their thoughts.

As luck would have it, the barracks was literally around the corner from Hotel Sandbank where they were staying. 'We can see if the commanding officer is available to see us, and then take some tea and afternoon snacks,' thought Harris, who was beginning to feel the first pangs of hunger.

They reached the barracks gates to find a sentry guarding the building. The soldier looked bored and tired, and was leaning heavily against his sentry box; there were cigarette butts scattered on the ground around him, and he was certainly not at all the alert, smart military figure that anyone would have expected. His rifle was propped against the back of the box, pretty well out of sight of any enemy agents or invading armies; for the entire world he looked as if he was just about to fall off to sleep.

Chief Inspector Harris took one look at this very dishevelled so-called warrior, and almost exploded with anger at the slovenly way he was acting.

"My God, man, is this any way to represent your unit? Does your commanding officer know what a scruffy guard he has, projecting the image of the army? You are a mess! Where is your senior officer, and quick about it?"

"Sorry, sir," said the sentry as he jumped to attention, "who shall I say is here?"

"Chief Inspector Harris from the Plymouth constabulary, and two other officers, and jump to it!"

By now both Cutler and Border were more than a little shaken by the sharp way Harris had attacked this sentry. The soldier virtually leapt out of the box, even leaving his rifle still resting where he had left it in his haste to now appease the policemen. Cutler had never really seen his friend lose his temper like this before, and it made him feel surprised at how quickly he had come to that state, and how venomous his attack had been.

After about two minutes, the soldier ran back and retrieved his gun trying not to be too obvious about it. He was red faced with shame and fear.

"I am to take you to see Captain Ferguson, sir; if you would all be kind enough to step this way."

He led them into the rather cramped room that was also the drill hall; it was not more than about fifty feet by fifty feet. It had served the children well whose classroom it had once been, but for an army unit, it was really not adequate. A room off to the left side had a sign painted onto it, saying *Adjutant*; inside this small cubbyhole, seated at an even smaller desk, was the aging figure of Captain Ferguson. He was in his fifties, very overweight and bulging out of his uniform just about everywhere. His red pulsating face looked as if it was just about to explode as he looked up at the three police officers from some papers he had been reading.

"Thank you, Jenkins, that will be all. So, gentlemen, what can I do for you?" His voice was at least half an octave higher that one would have expected. And to the three officers he sounded more like a woman than a man.

The customary introductions were effected, and then John Cutler proceeded to explain in a vague, loose manner the reasons for their enquiries.

"Firstly, anything you tell us will be kept in secrecy, nothing you say will bring anything back to you or your unit here within the Territorial Army; er, what..., I am sorry, what sort of soldiers are you?" Cutler realised that he didn't even know what sort of army unit this was.

"We are part of the Territorial division, the army Catering Corps."

"Thank you. As I was saying," Cutler paused again, but this time to cross his fingers behind his back, "nothing you say will be repeated by us. Where was I? Ah, yes. Can you tell me if there was a camp around this area recently for a part of the Royal Marines?"

Ferguson looked bewildered, and answered with a very puzzled frown on his forehead.

"I thought you were here to ask about us, not the Marines. Yes, there was a camp not far from here on Horsey Island. But they weren't there long, the rumour that went around was that they were training for a landing invasion, though, I hasten to add, this was all guesswork; nobody from their outfit came here for any reason, but it was like the Chinese whisper, one person says one thing and before you know it a sonata has turned into a symphony. I really don't know anything else, and I don't know of anyone that would know anything. What has happened, er, Inspector Cutler? Can you tell me anything?"

"Sorry, Captain, I cannot divulge what has happened and I don't want that Chinese whisper to start here, so less said soonest mended. Horsey Island, you say; how can we get there?"

"Drive around to Walton-on-the-Naze, and you should be able to get someone there to take you across."

Harris chipped in at this time. "Do you know of any bird watching groups in the area?"

The Captain's face now lit up, this was an area of special interest to him. "Bird watching, ah! Yes, there are at least two clubs that go bird watching, probably more, but I know of two. One is called 'Bird Watching and Painting for the Beginner', and can be found in Greek Street; I think they meet on Thursday evenings and go out weekends. I seriously thought of joining them myself: I love our feathered friends. The other one I know of is a private club run by some old men who collect the eggs; that is not what would interest me. I am not sure where and when they meet."

"Captain Ferguson, you have been a great help to us and I thank you. I am sorry for the mystery, but I do urge that nobody knows of our coming here, we don't want tongues wagging, do we?" Cutler turned to Harris. "Is there anything else you would like to ask?"

"No, Inspector, I think we can leave the Catering Corps to get on with their business, don't you?"

As the three officers walked out of the building back towards their car, Private Jenkins stood to attention with his rifle at the slope and gave them a 'present arms'. Cutler and Border smiled as they walked past; Harris frowned deeply, rubbing at a sore feeling that had developed across his chest and mumbled something under his breath, just loud enough so that everyone heard something, but was not able to pick out any sentence. When back in the car and settling down to try and get comfortable, he told the other two what he was thinking.

"That little shit on duty, I would have thrown the book at him if I was his commanding officer; I don't care if they are amateur soldiers or not, I don't care if they are fighting men or Catering Corps, a guard on duty is a guard on duty. He represents whatever it is that he is guarding, he should be smart and alert at all times, not looking as if he had just fallen out of bed; boy, that made me mad!"

"Well, I think we saw that," chirped Cutler almost laughing at his Chief's outburst. "What about some tea and maybe a sandwich or two, on me?"

They drove around the corner, parked the car in front of their hotel, went into the dining room and ordered a pot of tea for three and enough sandwiches to feed an army.

'Maybe that bloody Catering Corps has some sort of deal going with the hotel to make the food for its guests, because what I have seen up until now, I have not been impressed with.' Harris mused over this thought but did not seriously believe his own idea. He rubbed his chest once again, and then picked up his brew.

After they had finished their afternoon tea, it was starting to get dark, so it was decided between the three of them that they would continue their quest the next morning.

"Anyway," remarked Inspector Cutler, "I can now use the time to telephone Sergeant Maclean in Edinburgh, asking him to check out the Bird Watching groups, and see if they are missing a young female member."

50

"And I ought to telephone the Chief Constable in Plymouth, give some sort of report, and explain why we are going to be a day or two more before returning home."

Harris had become used to the ache across his rib cage, but rubbed it once again for luck.

The next morning the two policemen rose early from their beds, and presented themselves for breakfast at exactly eight o'clock. The waiter beamed from ear to ear: it was as if what had been said the day before had stuck in these two men's minds, and they had arrived for their morning food at a sensible time. 'After all,' he thought, 'I did give them a serious dressing down yesterday, it must have been taken on board.'

Kippers were on the menu, something that neither of the two West Country policemen had ever experienced before. Kippers, then porridge. They both hurried through the eating process, both acquired nasty indigestion from the two bloaters that they had eaten; Chief Inspector Harris's stomach hurt from the food and he was now prone to belching.

"Crickey, John, those kippers have given me terrible colic." And at that he created yet another burp, but one that was felt not heard. On going outside to take the air, and to see if PC Border was waiting, which he was, John Cutler looked up at the morning's sky; a beautiful warm day presented itself to them, and the air was clean and fresh. Harris was quick to enjoy the feeling of peace and tranquillity on stepping into that slightly salty sea air; yet he still managed to burp again, this time not trying to conceal it.

"Good morning, Sirs; I trust you spent a pleasant evening and feel perfectly refreshed to tackle yet another day?"

"My goodness, Eric, you are bright and snappy this day. Lost a penny and found a shilling?" joked Cutler, while Harris was still managing to bring up yet more air from his stomach.

"Something much better, sir; I went to see the man that runs the Bird Watching group after I left you two yesterday afternoon, and he remembers our girl Wendy Bryant. She was a member of the group and was liked and respected by one and all. I'm going to take you both over to his home right now to meet him. His name is Dominic Porter, a nice enough man, works as a grocer, owns his own shop, only a small one; fancies himself as being an entrepreneur, buys and sells properties amongst other things; as we say, he chivvies and spivs; but he comes across rather on the weak side, being spineless, lacking backbone; he is the sort that agrees with everyone, not wanting or daring to offend anyone. As soon as I spoke about Wendy, he went quite flushed and assured me that he was a perfectly respectable man and would never ever perpetrate such an appalling crime; he insisted on showing me just where he was on the day that Wendy died, even though he is not a suspect. I know that he has never been prosecuted for any crime: I had him checked out before I went to see him."

"This journey has been a revelation to both Inspector Cutler and me. We have been lucky enough to see policemen carrying out their duties, and beyond. Everyone, without exception, has treated us with due respect and courtesy; I am not sure our own force would have been so diligent to guest police officers." But he knew deep down they would have been.

They found the much shaken Dominic Porter sitting at his dining table, looking very wan and rather terrified. He calmed a little when Chief Inspector Harris offered him his hand, but though a faint smile appeared on his face, he was still as pale as a ghost; to the three police officers' eyes he looked what they knew he wasn't... guilty!

"Please, Mr. Porter, relax, we are here for your help; we don't believe for a minute that you had anything to do with Wendy Bryant's demise, you didn't, did you?" scowled Harris, really rather teasing the nervous, somewhat pathetic, middle-aged, plump, balding man that sat before them.

"Er... Officer Harris, I hardly knew the girl: she joined our little club about six months before that terrible murder happened. She never missed an outing, and her drawings and paintings were always of the very best quality."

"Well," interrupted Cutler, "for someone who barely knew her, you have already told us a great deal. Now, please, start from the beginning, the very day she came to join you bird watchers, or when you maybe saw her or met her before?" He took a deep breath, and then added, "Please relax, we are here as said before not to interrogate you, but to glean information, things we don't know about her."

Finally, Porter sighed deeply, and colour started to come back to his cheeks once more.

"Well, to start with, I had never seen her around before she appeared at one of our meetings. She might well have stood next to me from time to time, but I never noticed; so as far as I am concerned, she came into the group's life, as I said about six months before her death. She was a rather young girl, very innocent and extremely naïve in her mannerisms, but terribly enthusiastic about her skill with crayons and watercolours; her paintings and drawings were sometimes the best I have seen. To tell the truth," and now he was completely relaxed, "I often felt quite jealous of her abilities, but not enough to take her life," he hurriedly added.

"Did she mix with other members of the group?" asked Cutler in an almost buoyant tone of voice.

"Not until she met our newest member, a Mr. Michael Hart. He told us that he made musical instruments, string basses, I think he said, but he too loved to paint in his spare time. He came a couple of times after her sad demise, but then said that he had decided to move to London as there wasn't enough work in this area for him."

"So did Wendy make some attachment to this Michael Hart fellow?" asked an almost excited Cutler.

"She did seem to take a liking to him, but I have no idea as to whether they got any more intimate than just having the same interest in ornithology."

"And this Michael Hart, do you have an address for him, either in London or his old home here?" enquired Harris.

"Well, sadly, no. It is all very informal, we get to know one another, and you see people you know from the group around the town, so news gets passed that way." Then while pausing to breathe, he moved what little hair he had left away from his forehead, rubbed his chin and added, "It was strange that no one had ever met Hart before, and no one ever saw him around and about. I never thought about it before, but he was rather mysterious; after all Harwich is not a huge place."

"Tell us about your Mr. Hart. How old is he, is he well kept, fat, thin, bald, masses of hair, what sort of clothing did he wear? Could he in fact have been a soldier?" Harris frowned as he looked at Cutler and thought to himself, 'Oh, John, you should not have asked about being a soldier, that was more than a leading question; it should not have been asked, at least not yet.'

Porter thought long and hard about the question, and then replied with, "I would have thought he would have been anything from late twenties to early forties, hard to tell for sure. He spoke like a knowledgeable person; in fact I thought from the way he spoke that he was very intelligent. He certainly didn't have an Essex accent, though where he came from was hard to say, maybe more London, even South London, if I can be so bold. He was always smartly dressed, in fact sometimes overdressed for trips out where one might get muddy, but he invariably carried a bag with clean, smartly pressed brown overalls, which I assumed he used for his instrument making. But one could wonder why they were always pressed and so clean, not that I wondered at the time. He wasn't fat, more lean and healthy, always well groomed with dark black hair. As to being a soldier, I think not, as I asked him why he wasn't in the army and his reply was he wanted to join but had been turned down on medical grounds, which I never gave another thought to. Gentlemen, would you like some tea?"

"Well," butted in Constable Border, "that would be very nice, thank you."

When Porter left the room to make the tea, Border followed up his last words with, "We have now made him feel completely at ease and may need his help later on, specifically I, may be able to garner yet more details."

"Anyway, you really wanted a cup of tea, right?" chirped in Cutler with a broad grin, stretching from ear to ear.

"He has given us much to work on, so after tea, it's off to the old encampment."

They thanked Mr. Porter for his help and his hospitality, and then made their way around the south side of the town and out onto the road to Walton-on-the-Naze. The sky had started to cloud over, and for the first time in a couple of weeks it was starting to look like rain; what is more the temperature had definitely dropped a few degrees and both the West Country officers where starting to wish they had brought some extra clothing after all. By the time they reached the hamlet of Walton-on-the-Naze, it had started to drizzle with now quite strong winds, coming from the North West, obviously working up from nothing to gale force, much to the chagrin of the two officers, but not to Border's as he went everywhere quite prepared for fast weather changes: after all this was North Essex! By driving around Walton, they soon found what they were looking for. An old medieval tower loomed out of the swirling rain, with a huge barrier straight across the track leading to it. There, in front of them, was a sentry box and hut along with an armed soldier who raised his rifle in challenge as they approached.

After introducing themselves they were ushered into a small compound that could not be seen from the track they had taken, but it led them to the office that Captain Loveday was sitting in. He looked startled at the appearance of the sentry and the three civilians, placed the paperwork that he had been attending to down, and then almost leapt from his chair.

"Who are you and what are you doing here? This is restricted War Department land; you are not allowed to be here." He almost screamed at the soldier, "You will be in trouble for allowing civilians onto this post."

"Sir," protested the luckless sentry, "they are police officers and it is important that they speak to you."

With this information Captain Loveday calmed down considerably, and then offered the strangers a chance to state their reasons for breaking into W.D. property. Chief Inspector Harris told the Captain all about the murders, omitting to add that he thought that the perpetrator might well be a member of the Royal Marine Corps; instead he was wondering if there had been any Marines on this base at the time of this particular event as someone might know something. None of it sounded very convincing but it seemed to work. Captain Loveday thought long and hard, and then added completely off the record that there *had* been a detachment of Marines here around the dates given, but none had been allowed off base as they were there on special duties, and he couldn't possibly tell civilians what they had been up to. When asked if he, the Captain, knew of any Marine that might have been interested in ornithology, his answer was swift and to the point.

"I have already stated, no one would have been allowed off this base, no one! But there is plenty of interesting bird life to be found around these parts, and there are lots of soldiers that follow bird watching as a hobby. More than that I cannot say."

"Thank you, Captain Loveday, you have told us all we need to know. Oh, just one more little thing. Where did they go after leaving here, if you are not disclosing official secrets?"

"There is no secret where they then went; they left to go to Plymouth!"

The very next day, packed and ready for their journey back to the West Country, both Harris and Cutler shook the hand of Constable Eric Border very warmly, as they had learnt to like this younger man very much indeed.

"You will go far in the force, and if it doesn't happen for you here, remember John Cutler and myself; we will get you down to the more pleasant climate and countryside of Plymouth, we need men like you."

"That is extremely nice of you to say that, sir; let me know what is happening concerning our man, and in the meantime I shall interview the rest of the bird group to see if I can add yet more. It has been a pleasure knowing you both. Just one last thing; I hope you are not offended in any way, but my wife made some sandwiches for your journey back to London and onwards, just in case it is hard to buy anything on the train or at stations. And I recently brewed up a lot of country wine, so I brought you two bottles of mead; it might help the sandwiches go down."

"You are extremely kind," remarked a very happy looking Inspector Cutler, "we are not offended in any way at all!"

The train pulled out of the station more or less on time. Cutler and Harris sat on their respective seats and started to laugh, and for a long while both of them would break out into spontaneous laughter; they didn't quite know why they were laughing, but they both felt that they should.

"We will nail the bastard, I know we will!" said Harris tucking into a cheese and homemade pickle sandwich.

"This is the first time since poor Cynthia's death that I feel we are now looking at the home run, and are we going to knock that for a sixer!"

They both grinned again, and this time took great swigs from their bottle of mead.

"God almighty! This stuff is far too sweet for my palate!" choked Chief Inspector Harris. Again they both laughed heartily.

VI

Harris had been away from his wife for seven days now, and they were both very glad to see one another again. He had looked forward to the trip very much, but he always missed his wife when she was not around, she was his rock, and he knew it. After they had kissed and Harris had patted their overweight and aging Labrador on his head, they stood back from one another. Barbara studied him and spoke in a rather subdued manner.

"Steven, you look awful. I thought you two were going to have a relaxed trip, you needed a rest, and you look as if you have run all the way from London, and carried a package as well."

"Oh, I'm alright, but I have had a great deal of bad indigestion; we ate kippers the other day for breakfast, and I suffered for twenty-four hours with nonstop belching; it was very unpleasant and it gave me a nasty pain across my chest; that pain comes and goes quite a bit, but it's nothing to worry about."

Barbara was not convinced, but knew better than to argue with her man; she just sighed quietly to herself in that knowing way, and sat down and listened to what news he had for her.

"Our original thoughts were correct, and though we still don't know who did these awful crimes, we are ninety percent sure that it is a member of the Royal Marines. Of course, now they have left Plymouth, so I am going to have to find out where they are based at the moment. Their commanding officer will have to do some sharp talking; I always thought that if a soldier is confined to barracks, he will find a way out if he wants to. And I am sure that whatever his name is will turn up sooner or later. I am taking the rest of this day off, so that I can write up my reports for the Commissioner, then I am going to put myself in gear and weed out this piece of scum, if it's the last thing I ever do."

Steven was quick to notice that as soon as he felt renewed agitation concerning this case, his chest started to hurt once more. 'I must keep myself calm, not overdo it, and no one must know that my problem is getting more serious.' He knew he was suffering from angina, and he knew that if he did not slow down he would not reach retirement, which is what he yearned for most of all. 'After all, who wants to spend their life around the dregs of humanity?' The job had seemed rewarding for many years, but as he grew older, the cases seemed to grow worse, more complicated and more violent.

He missed his sons very much and wondered what they were up to. He had received a letter a few weeks previously from his oldest son Michael, along with cuttings from the *Dover Post* telling the story of how his patrol boat had managed to rescue the entire crew of a German U-boat: they had caught it in their searchlights one night, and they had shelled it until it was starting to sink; all the crew had leapt into the sea, but they had managed to pull them all out and bring them back to Dover harbour for interrogation. For their bravery and humanity, the entire crew of the patrol boat was awarded the Distinguished Service Medal, and there they were, Michael in the middle of the photograph, being presented to the First Sea Lord, Sir John Jellicoe. Chief Inspector Steven "Knocker" Harris felt the pride again swell up inside him at the memory and longed for the day when he would see his two sons again, under better circumstances. He wanted to see the war end, get retired, move into a smaller and warmer house, and have his family once more around the hearth. He was adamant that the two lads should now be married and creating yet more Harrises to fill the country with.

'Never mind all this melancholy dribble, time to write that report, we have a villain to catch and hang.'

Next morning, feeling completely refreshed and with a new spring in his step he presented himself back to the station, where Inspector Cutler was anxiously waiting for him.

"I have been waiting for you for an hour now, you are never late; had you not come in five minutes I was going to send a Constable to see if you were alright. I wrote my report last night as I expect you did too. But I have already heard on the grapevine that the powers that be are not at all pleased with us for being away so long. I am waiting to hear that we have also overspent our budget upon this case. It makes me sick when I think how well we have done."

Immediately Harris felt the sharp pain across his chest again. 'Slow yourself down; so far it is just rumour, nothing else.' But rumour soon turns into fact as a raging Chief Constable Jolly came storming into view.

"And what the hell have you two been up to?" he almost screamed.

"Sir, we have had a very successful trip, it has been worth the time and the extra money. We are now very close to making an arrest," jumped in Harris.

"Well, who is he then? Name names."

"Sir, we don't as yet have a name but we are very sure that it was a soldier from the Royal Marines that perpetrated these awful murders. We wish to visit their new barracks and try and wheedle their commanding officer into helping us, instead of blocking, as I believe he might. In the meantime, I suggest you read both our reports, and very carefully." His tone of voice had dropped and this made Jolly even more angry, as he considered Harris's attitude to be confrontational: he was almost blowing a head gasket with rage; but no more words came from his mouth, just venom. He held out his hand to take both the reports, and as the two Inspectors started for the door, he hurled a final cascade of words at them... "These had better be good, or you will both be for the high jump. And you are both too bloody old to be out of work!"

Harris and Cutler moved out of the office, commandeered a car and started for the old barracks. When they reached their destination the gates were still open, as yet another body of soldiers had taken the place of the Marines: it was the Royal Artillery. After presenting themselves to the guard on duty, they were taken forthwith to see the duty officer. There they presented their case in its broader terms, leaving out what they suspected, and merely requesting help from the marines.

'So, where did they go on leaving here,' wondered Cutler, and asked just that question. At first the duty officer declined to answer, but with some serious persuading from the two police officers, he admitted that he knew they had left to take up position within the castle at Dover. They thanked him for his help, and then proceeded to first drive back to the station to make sure that they still had jobs, then on to Dover, with hopefully the Chief Constable's blessing. The latter was deep in thought when they entered his office, yet another drab pokey hole which would have made a better stores room than an interview room for the Chief. He looked up, placed the report down that he had been perusing, and in a much more conciliatory voice said:

"I have read most of your report, Harris, and if what you both say is correct, then maybe the time and money were well spent. I am sorry for my outburst earlier. But there is absolutely no excuse for not keeping me well informed."

"Yes, I can see that. But things moved at a great pace, and we just had to go with the flow of the tide. Can I please tell you what we have found out?" But before there was an answer he continued, "Now we have discovered that the Royal Marines have moved into the castle at Dover, I would like your permission to try once more to gleam some information out of their commanding officer." Harris looked for support from Cutler, but it was not needed. "Actually, sir, I would like to borrow a car and a driver; it might give us a little weight when we arrive, at least it will look for all the world that we mean business."

"Oh, just go and do what you have to." Then the Chief paused a moment and added, "You know, we might need some government support for this case."

At this last remark a surprised look registered upon Harris's and

Cutler's faces. He carried on, "If the commanding officer pulls the official secret acts upon you two, we will need special help to get this completely sorted, done and dusted."

They walked out of Chief Constable Jolly's office, now more confused than when they had entered, but at least their jobs were safe.

"Before we go to Dover, what about a cup of char?" but before Harris could answer, Cutler hailed PC Williams. "Williams, two teas, strong and sweet. And now please!"

"Williams," enquired Harris as he sipped his piping hot brew, "are you busy for the next couple of days?"

"Well, I have some reports to write, and I have a pickpocket in the holding cells awaiting my pleasure to charge and question him. Other than that, things are extremely quiet." This attempt at wit had fallen on deaf ears; neither of the two Inspectors listened to anything he said.

"Good," said Harris again, "you can drive Inspector Cutler and me east along the coast to Dover." Then turning to Cutler he added, "You are right, if we turn up looking official, it might give us an edge."

. It took them the entire next day to drive the two hundred and fifty odd miles to the town of Dover. If they ever thought Plymouth was busy, then they hadn't reckoned on Dover. There was an incredible amount of army transport everywhere, with many road blocks checking who they were, and what they wanted. Other than in the old town, there were precious few civilians to be seen anywhere, nothing but the military prevailed in the streets. It took another hour to find a hotel with bed space for the three of them. But in the end they were lucky to find an old inn, which also served food. All three were extremely tired from the long drive across, and were soon contemplating a good night's sleep. They finished their food, drank their drinks and wearily climbed the stairs to their respective bedrooms. They rose early, had breakfast and were ready to meet whatever challenge; when they reached the castle, they were prepared, or so they thought, for the next hurdle in their case.

At the entrance to the castle grounds, they faced several concrete road obstacles, then a wooden barrier where a sentry box was standing. They were challenged by a guard whose rifle was trained upon them. Cutler glanced at Harris; both men were shaken at the soldier's purposeful stance, conveying that if provoked, he would without a second thought, pull the trigger.

"We are here to see your commanding officer," stated Harris after asserting who they were and where they had come from; this was to make sure there was no misunderstanding from the sentry.

"Pull this vehicle over to the side so that army transport can get through without cars blocking their way, then wait in the car until I say otherwise. Is that understood?" He was only a young soldier, not more than eighteen years of age, but they quickly pulled their car over to the side, and sat in it quite passively. After what must have been forty minutes, the sentry returned, looking just as stern as before, still keeping his gun pointing in their general direction.

"There is no way you will be seeing any commanding officer, but a Major Gleeson has agreed to give you all a few minutes of his time. Leave the car here, give me the keys, and follow the Corporal over there; he is doing the honours for you."

"Thank you, Private, you can put that gun down and out of our faces now; we are on the same side, you know." Harris was starting to get annoyed again, and his rib cage was beginning to get that far too familiar feeling of tightness.

Major Gleeson was another soldier who had seen better days. He was approximately fifty years of age, but being completely bald and large, not in height but in girth, he really looked at least ten years older. He sweated profusely and the acrid smell was beginning to permeate the whole office. He did not bother to stand up when the three policemen entered, feeling that they obviously did not merit respect, and anyway they should not even be there. He had never been abroad which meant he had never seen action, and for him now it was sadly too late. He was bitter, and he did not care who knew it. Gleeson vented his spleen at anyone he thought would not be in a position to retaliate.

"Yes, gentlemen, what can I do for you?" But he immediately went back to his paperwork while Inspector Cutler tried to explain that they knew a small detachment of the marines were now stationed within the castle walls, and they would deem it a great favour if they could speak to their commanding officer.

"Who is that officer?" enquired an indifferent Gleeson.

"Well, that's the problem; we don't know who he is. Maybe you can look up your records and tell us?" snapped Harris, now starting to feel very off colour.

"Well, then, I cannot help you. You must make a request in writing, and then I will see what can be done."

"For God's sake, man," bellowed a now extremely angry Harris, "we have come all the way from Plymouth to interview him, and you say we are wasting our time. Oh, I shall be writing for sure, and I will make certain that everybody knows who has held us up in our enquiries."

"This is not a shoplifting offence, we are talking about a triple murder, and if we don't stop the villain who has committed these gruesome crimes, he will strike again. Do you want an extra murder on your conscience?" At this Cutler banged the table the Major was sitting at really hard, and this made the Major jump almost out of his seat.

"Guard!" shouted Gleeson. The sentry, who had been standing outside all the time, came in bearing his rifle once again.

"Guard, show these gentlemen back to their vehicle, and make sure that they leave the area, or arrest them all and we will see what a military tribunal will have to say about their appalling behaviour."

"Oh, we are going alright, and I know your name is Major Gleeson; sadly I suspect you could be leaving this man's army rather more quickly than you were hoping for!"

Much to the horror of Harris the sentry now made sure that a bullet was in the gun. They were therefore much relieved once they had settled into their car, turned it around and left Dover castle.

"You look very pale, Steven, are you alright?"

"I will be, John, but that bastard really annoyed me; what a disgrace this man is! Let's get back to Plymouth; we can do no more good here."

"Just one thing, Steven, before we leave; let's go and see the local constabulary and inform them that they have a potential murderer on their patch. We can, with their help, keep up to speed on this case."

They visited the local police chief who turned out to be a decent sort of chap, and knew of Gleeson.

"Should anything strange happen here concerning young girls, I will be straight in touch with you both down in the West Country. In the meantime just relax; you have done all you can here. You have learned a salutary lesson: the armed forces are laws unto themselves, but there is more than one way to 'skin a killer', army or not! Have a safe journey home."

"Thank you, Inspector Riley, we will do our best; hopefully we will meet again in the not too distant future."

The journey back to Plymouth was slow but uneventful; they actually didn't reach their respective homes until nearly two-thirty the next morning. There had been a great deal of military traffic on all the coastal roads.

"I suggest we three meet back at the station at one o'clock this afternoon; it will give us time to rest and write those bloody reports. We want Chief Constable Jolly to be very much on our side; we need his sort of clout to get within Dover's hallowed walls." Harris then turned to PC Williams. "Williams, you have been a brick, a breeze of fresh air. In fact I cannot remember a PC being so quiet; it must be some sort of record."

Cutler laughed, then added this own rendition.

"Don't you listen to him, Williams, it was a pleasure being driven by someone who didn't aim the vehicle but drove it!" He then bowed in a grand gesture.

"It has been my pleasure, sirs, anytime." Then he bowed back.

'Cheeky young pup,' thought Harris, as yet again he rubbed his ribs.

Harris and Cutler sat patiently in the office, awaiting their chief's pleasure. After a few minutes his head bobbed up from the reports, and then he scowled hard at the two Inspectors.

"So, run out of that old Harris-Cutler luck, eh? Now you need my assistance, eh?" He paused, took a breath, timed to increase the tension in the two men, and then continued. "But with a following wind and my help, between us we will get this case closed to all our satisfactions. I shall now write my own report, but this time it will be addressed to the Home Secretary in Whitehall. When in doubt, go straight to the man at the top. But you two will have to be a little patient; this will take some time. So now let me get on with my work, and when it is done, I will give you both a copy of my letter to him. Both of you must have a stack of unfinished business to attend to, that I am quite sure of. Oh, before you leave, what was the name of the officer at the castle, I'll make sure that his hindrance is well publicised."

For once, he knew Chief Constable Jolly was right: letters to the Home Secretary should produce the result that was needed, plus time away from this stressful case should make him more relaxed. 'There had to be a first time!' thought Harris. 'Anyway it is going to be a pleasure not thinking about those dreadful slayings. Normal work will be a nice change.'

Jolly's letter was a fine example of the benefits of a higher education. It was addressed to the Home Secretary and copies sent to other important personages within the government, calling on all the help he could muster. He explained in a circumspect manner how three murders had occurred around the country, all with similar characteristics. He also implied cautiously that it just happened that the same unit of Royal Marines had been in the area each time, and as it was extremely hard to get any information from the unit's officers, it had left them feeling powerless, which was the reason for the letter. Anyway, it would be better if the commanding officer was ordered to assist the police, with the obvious aim of keeping civilians onside; besides, if the facts came to the knowledge of the gutter press, they would have a field day. It was that last sentence that both Cutler and Harris thought would do the trick.

Harris went back to normal duties, robberies, stabbings, rape and pillage. 'Oh, to be in the norm again! Villains from the West Country, I love you! At least now I won't have a heart attack.' And he didn't.

*The breach created as a result of the explosion from 10,000 kilos of high explosives aboard the "C-3",
a British submarine.*

British mine sweepers used in the raid.

The British torpedo boat"Thetis". It sunk at the entrance to the canal at Zeebrugge.

The British ships "Intrepid" and "Iphigenir" scuttled to block the canal at Zeebrugge. This strategy proved ineffective because German submarines were able to manoeuvre around the hulks.

The furthest point of the Mole where you can see the lighthouse, what was left of the German guns. The profile of SS "Brussels" is visible above the water level where she was sunk.

Remains of "Vindictive" which sank in front of the harbour close to the German guns.

VII

When Lieutenant Bartlett finally returned with his men back to the barracks after their march around the Plymouth coastal areas, he went straight to his room where he kept his personal chest always locked. He painstakingly opened the locks, making sure that no one was about to enter his domain. He withdrew his '*Katana*' Samurai sword and the '*Shoto*' dagger that went with it, once again very carefully cleaned both weapons, then took an emery paper and started his usual routine of sharpening. This would always take thirty minutes for each blade, and each blade was so sharp that it would cut through cloth that had just been dropped onto it. He loved his blades: such fine steel; everyone talked about Sheffield steel, but he knew there was nothing in Sheffield that would ever match these beauties. He polished and caressed them as if he was pampering a pet cat, then placed them back on their appointed rack and very carefully placed the rack back in the chest. Standing up he looked down once more at his pride and joy, then closed the lid and locked it. Moving to the mirror he studied the image staring back at him and thought, 'I should be taking my shower and dressing for dinner.' He looked fit and healthy, he felt great. Life was certainly treating him well.

Later, after dinner had been served and ingested, and their commanding officer, Colonel Chartiers, was making a few toasts with the port, ending with the King's health, he then asked for silence from all the officers, requested that all other personnel leave the room, and ordered that the doors be locked as what he had to say was now top secret.

"Gentlemen, if I may have your attention! Many of you here enlisted before or at the opening of hostilities with the foe. None of you have yet seen action! Well, sirs, that is soon to change."

With these remarks the officers came alive and all moved onto the edge of their chairs, as if this action would make them hear better. You could have heard a pin drop. The very walls, furniture and paintings seemed to stand to attention and listen with bated breath to every word that the commanding officer was uttering.

"As you are all well aware, things have not been going particularly well on any of our fronts with the enemy, in fact the only saving grace is that the conditions are equally as bad for the Central Powers. But in the sea war we are faring extremely badly: German submarines are making a mockery of our shipping and we are losing more ships than we can ever hope to build. The Kaiser brags openly that it takes the British three months to make a ship and the U-boats three minutes to sink it! Sadly, gentlemen, the top brass agree with him. These are indeed desperate times and unless we can alter that statement we will not be able to continue the war into 1918 or onwards. We are surely on the edge of defeat."

There was a lot of shuffling of feet, as the congregated officers started to feel very uncomfortable and downright useless, if not to say redundant. What had all these years of training been for, was the general thought running through unnerved minds.

"It is time to put a stop to the U-boat problem or admit defeat, and I really don't think anyone of us will tolerate that, will we?"

There was a lot of mumbling, then a general rising of voices which ended in all thirty officers standing and demanding the right to fight the enemy. Of course this was exactly the reaction that Colonel Chartiers had hoped for, but he concealed the wry smile that had started to spread across his mouth.

"It seems, gentlemen, that a plan has been put forward which will include us; what it is, I do not know as yet; but all leave is cancelled from now on. The various training exercises that we have undertaken around the country seem to be rehearsals for what we will be doing, and as I hear more, so will you. Needless to say, everything is top secret, and that means," at this, he leant forward and banged his fist down hard on the table, "no telling wives, sweethearts, mothers, fathers, or even father confessors. Though the men will soon become aware that things are starting to happen, they, most of all, must know as little as possible, as they talk even in their sleep."

There was a small ripple of laughter that went around the table after that quip.

"One last thing I can tell you is that we will almost certainly be moving on from here within a very short space of time. Prepare your-selves, and prepare your men. It is time for some of us to become heroes, hopefully."

Again, a ripple of laughter followed.

"So, gentlemen, this is the start of our fight, albeit when and where? I wish you all a good night and thank you for your hospitality."

All the men stood and saluted as Colonel Chartiers moved to the door and exited, leaving a smiling, bewildered bunch of men to make of that what they would.

"So finally, we might get to see some action," said Captain Williamson to the officer on his immediate left, which happened to be Lieutenant Bartlett. "I knew it would come; we haven't been doing all this training just to keep the men on their toes, I guessed it was leading to something big. So what is it?"

Bartlett smiled, which made his scar ripple over his left eye. He was feeling extremely pleased with himself. He was one officer that was comprehensively prepared, and all the hard work that he had put his men through made him totally convinced that they and he were capable of anything the War Office threw at them.

"I feel as if I have been waiting for this my whole life; just to know that these years have not been wasted is good enough for now. As to what it is we are going to be doing? Well, it must be something to do with the U-boat scourge, which is why we have been training on landing from boats onto beaches, and storming sea defences and harbours. I'd give a week's pay betting that I am right."

"Well, I for one won't be taking that wager; I believe you are probably correct; but which sea defences, which harbour?" Williamson grabbed the port bottle as it was being passed around from his right side, poured himself a generous helping then remembered Bartlett. "Want a refill, old boy?"

"No thank you, Captain, from now on I am signing the pledge." His voice raised in pitch a little, but noticeably enough. "No alcohol until we have something to celebrate: I am going to be totally prepared for any eventuality, and what is more, I shall make sure that my men are in the same state of preparedness as I am. Whatever it is we do, we will storm it!" At this he brought the palm of his left hand heavily down on the table, which rattled a few glasses and stopped everyone in their tracks. There was a moment's silence; then a cheer started from his fellow officers which made Bartlett turn bright red. They laughed; he then caught the mood, and matched their laughter.

"Sorry, gentlemen, I got quite carried away then. I think it is time to depart; I want to finish a watercolour of a moorhen in flight that I started the other day." Bartlett then went on, "I shall leave the fist banging and speculating to you worthy officers and the more mundane pleasures of life to me." With this, he took a deep bow, and started for the door. Cheering followed him out of the dining room, much to his satisfaction.

"He is a very decent fellow, a gentleman," declared Captain Williamson to the officer on this right hand side.

"And his men love him; they would follow him to hell and back. I wish I commanded the same respect as Bartlett does," came the reply.

The next morning turned out to be rather cold and dull, with a definite feeling that rain was going to be following on not far behind. Bartlett rose early, washed fastidiously, smartened himself, had early breakfast, then went onto the parade ground to talk to his NCOs, and help drill the men. He knew he looked every inch the gentleman; he wanted to make sure that his men knew he would always look like a million dollars, and that he expected them to look and act the same way; he generally got what he wanted. The Sergeants and Corporals always tended to let him down, but from now on he was going to change their rather slovenly ways. He wanted men at the top of their fitness, especially men who were in authority; he would start to make them jump when he spoke; things were most definitely going to alter. And to prove his point he would never ask anyone to do what he would not, so it was going to be hard for everyone.

The Sergeants went through their normal routine: nothing very strenuous there. 'Time to up the tempo,' he thought.

"Sergeant Laker, Sergeant Riley, would you kindly come over here, please." Bartlett and his two rather overweight Sergeants walked just a little way across the parade ground, just out of earshot from any listening Private.

"From now on, Sergeants, we are all going to take a more active role in the drill, exercise and training. We have all allowed ourselves to become complacent and more than a little rotund." At this, Bartlett patted his own flat muscular stomach, if only to spare the blushes of his Sergeants. "We all need to get in trim. I am going to let you both into a secret, but please keep it to yourselves. We are finally going into action, and we must all perform to the best of our ability. I know nothing more than what I have told you," holding up his hands in a gesture of submission, "but something is in the air, and we have been warned to expect to be on the move. When we go over the top, or do whatever we are picked to accomplish, I want to make sure that when I take one hundred and twenty-eight men, three Corporals and two Sergeants in, I bring that same number out. Fitness, that is what we need, and I am relying on you two to make me fitter, and of course the men and Corporals as well." He didn't specify the two of them, but he knew he had made the point. "So, gentlemen, let's get back on that parade ground and really begin to work out... *all* of us!"

They started with an hour's worth of close order drill then it was followed up with racing contests to find out who the best runners were. Two stood out: one Private Worth and one Corporal McGhee, a very burly Glaswegian who sported a broken nose, a row of missing teeth, and a jaw that was about as square as it could be. McGhee had known more than a few brawls in his life. But he was so fast at running he outpaced almost everyone, surprising all as most were half his age. Bartlett made a note of the two names. 'They might make good runners if needed,' he thought. Bartlett made sure that Laker and Riley competed in all routines, as he also did. Yet he always managed never to win any races, making it appear that the men were better than him; but deep down he knew he could outrun *any* of them.

"Sergeant!" Bartlett called to Laker. "Lunch, I think. Time to take the men into the canteen and feed their hungry bodies; but please make sure they wash first. Clean hands and clean minds." He of course joked, but yet again the men complied. "After a hearty meal, we are going to take a turn at storming those Norman ramparts," he announced, pointing in the direction of the Roman lighthouse, near the Norman walls.

Day after day they trained and worked out. Both Sergeant Laker and Sergeant Riley had lost several pounds in weight, and were now able to keep pace with their men and their Lieutenant. What is more they all felt so much better. Riley had even stopped smoking, while Laker had cut down to less than ten a day. They only drank beer, and never more than two pints a night. Times and men were changing. It did not take long before all the Battalion were aware of Bartlett's unit and how well they were achieving what was asked of them; they were leading the way, and by a long chalk. Bartlett was proud of his men, Sergeants Laker and Riley were proud of what they had become, the Corporals and Privates were glad that they led the field within the Battalion. Not only was Bartlett at peak performance, but so were his entire unit. Their gunnery training left a wide gap between them and their nearest rival unit. The rate of shots that each soldier could fire accurately with his 303 Lee Enfield rifle was winning them plaudits from all the other officers, so it was not long before Colonel Chartiers was also talking about his man, Lieutenant Bartlett.

Christmas came, and the English winter had set in with a vengeance: rain, sleet, snow and cold, but most of all windy rain, the sort that penetrates through any clothing, making one extremely uncomfortable from the wet, cold conditions. Many of the Battalion's men had gone down with a particularly nasty form of influenza; in fact there had been several deaths, which were very worrying for the Colonel and the medical staff.

None of this affected Bartlett who had become a man with a mission. His men were now without exception the fittest Colonel Chartiers had ever seen.

"Corporal Jones," hailed Chartiers. "Please go and fetch Lieutenant Bartlett, I wish to talk to him."

"Sir, yes, sir, right away."

Five minutes later Bartlett was standing outside Colonel Chartiers' office awaiting the call to enter.

"Come in, Bartlett, don't stand on ceremony. Want tea or coffee?"

"Coffee, sir, I haven't had any coffee for several weeks; we seem to be unable to get it in the officers' mess."

There came a slightly embarrassed cough from Chartiers as he realised that he had procured all the remaining stock for his own office.

"Jones, fetch two cups of coffee, and make it quick, please."

"Sir, yes, sir, right away."

"Sit down, Lieutenant; this is an informal chat between you and me. Firstly I want to congratulate you on the strength and fitness of your men. It has been very impressive to watch the development of your training, and I have been watching, make no mistake about it.

As you know, there is something big brewing and we are all going to be a part of it; at least I hope all. But I want to know, from the horse's mouth so to speak, after so long in the Marines, how do you feel about going into combat now? You can speak your mind, anything you say will not leave this room; it is just that I feel strongly about officers who have seen no action being offered a way out. At this time of the war, with so many awful tragic battles going nowhere and leaving so many fine men dead or dying on the battlefield, I for one, feel the need to take stock before committing any more young men. So if you think it is time just for that desk job, I would understand perfectly well."

"Sir, thank you for your concern, but I know that I have never been readier, and I think I speak for all my men. I feel I was born to be a part of this war; I have waited patiently for the chance to see and fight the enemy, so I really cannot imagine not being able to do my duty."

"I am glad to hear you say that, Bartlett, but I had to ask, as the little skirmish that we are going to be involved with is going to be just for volunteers, no one will be press-ganged."

"Can you tell me anything about what we will be doing, sir?"

"Well, officially no, but off the record, I am going to explain a little of what it is about. We are going to send a small force of Marines to attack the moles at Zeebrugge and Ostend. With the Marines will be a submarine, which will be loaded to the gunnels with high explosives, rammed under the viaduct at Zeebrugge then blown up. There will also be some old ships which will be sunk in mid-channel so as to block the U-boats either in or out, thus hopefully ending their threat in the North Sea to our shipping. The Marines' job will be to capture the mole and hold it while the submarine and ships do their duty. There will be rescue ships to take all of you off the mole once the aims have been achieved. So, Lieutenant Bartlett, you now know as much as me. Obviously, all I have told you is top secret, so no discussing it with your unit, understood?"

"My God," said Bartlett, "I guessed that it would be something along these lines. Wow, I am really happy about being a part of this little adventure. When do we go, sir?"

"No idea, Lieutenant; you will just have to be patient. But you and the men that volunteer will be getting special training, oh, I think during the first week of January. Just tell your NCOs that something big is about to break and volunteers are asked for, and when you have selected in your mind which ones are going with you, ask your men the same question."

"Colonel, there is a call for you from the admiralty; can you come and take it outside please?" enquired Jones, always feeling nervous when asking his Colonel to leave the office because the blasted telephones were not working properly, and the only way outside calls came through was in the outer office.

"Excuse me, Bartlett; I will be as quick as possible." Chartiers rose and left his office following his faithful Jones.

The first thing that caught Bartlett's eye as he stood and looked around the office was headed paper from the police at Scotland Yard in London. He was transfixed at the glimpse of the heading, *Scotland Yard!* He knew he had to see this letter, which read:

```
...to inform Colonel Chartiers that he is to give assistance
in every possible way to the two police officers from Plymouth
constabulary during their investigations concerning the murders
of three females in areas where The Royal Marines are known to
have been in training. Colonel Chartiers is to grant permission
for the interviewing of all men, officers included. There is to
be no repeat of the hampering that seems to have occurred in
Plymouth. The good name of the Battalion depends on good cooperation
with all local police forces.
```

Bartlett felt shaken to the core; he went completely white and for a brief moment wobbled on his feet. He saw that it was signed by the Chief Superintendent of Scotland Yard, confirmed and agreed by the First Sea Lord himself. 'So they are catching up with me. Well, I will have my day, I will go on this adventure, maybe I just won't return!'

"What on earth is the matter with you, Bartlett; you have gone as white as a sheet." Colonel Chartiers had finished his telephone conversation and had come back into his own office to see Lieutenant Bartlett ashen and slightly shaky.

"Er, nothing, sir, I guess I must be hungry, and in need of something to drink."

"Well, my boy, you take care of yourself: you are going to be a major influence during this raid, your role could be pivotal, and so you must keep up the good work, and keep well." This last sentence was said more as an order than a wish leading the recipient to believe that the old man really cared. Bartlett was dismissed as easily as one would swat a fly and then forget all about it. But Bartlett didn't care; he was finally going to have his chance of being the hero he believed was his destiny.

"Sergeant Laker, Sergeant Riley. Would you both come with me to my office; I have to talk to you about something special. Get Corporal Tillingham to carry on with the exercise."

The three men entered the small room that Bartlett used as his office.

"Now what I am about to tell you is top secret, so not a word gets outside this office; is that understood?"

"Yes, sir!" came the reply from both the NCOs.

"Well, gentlemen, we are going to be finally given our chance to hit at the Boche. There is going to be a raid on Zeebrugge and Ostend to try and block the ports, thus stopping the submarines from using them. It will be our job to take the moles and hold them against counterattacks, while the navy sink some old ships to block the channels. But no one is being made to go, all must volunteer. So, what say you two? Will you both come on this adventure?"

There was a huge grin on David Bartlett's face: he was warming to the prospect of this pleasant little journey; the more he thought about it, the more he could see his destiny being fulfilled.

Riley looked at Laker and went slightly pale for a second or two. Laker was the first to respond.

"Tell the truth, sir, I had given up on ever doing any fighting. But, after all, isn't this the reason we all joined the army? Yes, sir, you can count on me, I will follow you anywhere, sir!"

"Well, sir, as for me, I must admit that you have given me a bit of a fright too. But any excuse for being away from the wife sounds good to me. Do you have any idea when all this is going to take place?"

"No idea at all, except that we can expect special training after the New Year. Now you both know why I made you two train as hard as the men. Neither of you have been as fit as you are now in several years, am I right?"

"What about the men, sir? Will we be taking them all?"

"Can't answer that one yet; I really don't know any more than I have told you; but I have been told that only volunteers will go, no one is being pressed into service. It will be very much up to the three of us who stays and who goes. So, let's monitor the training very carefully and see who are the best. If they are too old, or have too many problems, discount them; if there are men with several children to support, discount them too. We will weed out what we must; hopefully we have some time yet."

Bartlett looked out of the small window, wiped off the condensation and noted that the rain was even heavier than earlier.

"Well, gentlemen, it is time to start storming those walls again. Once more onto the mole my friends, once more onto the mole, we will fill the gaps with their dead and all before tea… eh?" All three men laughed heartily, old friends together.

Over the next couple of weeks Bartlett's unit worked really hard; all the men got to hear about the forthcoming raid. By telling the two Sergeants Bartlett knew that with the old Chinese whisper the news would travel. Out of the one hundred and twenty-eight enlisted men, only twelve were weeded out, mainly through being a little too old, or married with children to support. Much to Lieutenant Bartlett's annoyance, one of his Corporals was excused as he had contracted what was thought to be influenza. Bartlett went to the infirmary to visit, but was mortified when informed that Corporal Sparrow had died the night before. The doctor in charge was very concerned about the spreading of any infection, and asked Bartlett to have his entire unit assemble for the next morning, so that they could all be looked over for signs of the dreaded disease. Doctor Louis was a very thorough man and took nearly the whole day to examine the men. Bartlett kept all his fingers crossed, and knew that his fitness regime was working well, when at the end of a very worrying day, Bartlett and his men were given the all clear. 'Nothing is going to stop this moment of glory; nobody will take away my destiny!'

· That following Monday ten army trucks drew up at the barracks, just after six in the morning. Bartlett and his men were off to training for a few days; Sheerness was their destination, on the Isle of Sheppey. Not a hugely long journey, but a very uncomfortable one; after a drive of three hours, the solid-wheeled lorries fitted with plain wooden seating, driving over cobbled roads, left everyone feeling bruised and tired. They were to camp in a field in the little hamlet of Minster; there were several hundred other men there too. Everything was drenched; it was raining yet again, as it had been for the past week. All the soldiers, including their officers, were expected to pitch their own tents, make their own fires and generally look after themselves. The only attraction that Minster had was a small solitary pub, but officially that was off limits to all ranks except officers, and there were very few of them. Very quickly, with the help of the trusty Laker and Riley, the men were settled and fed. Bartlett withdrew a packet of *"Capstan Full Strength"* cigarettes, offered them around. The packet emptied without David getting a smoke himself, so he went straight to his rucksack, and this time, withdrew a packet of fifty. He got his smoke, but after the pack had done the rounds there were precious few left for him to enjoy, should he wish to. Bartlett knew what he was doing: 'never try and bribe the men, but be generous when things go well'. They loved him for it.

After an officers' briefing, it was time to settle the men down for the night. Heaven knew it was going to be wet and cold, but in their state of fitness it would be nothing to these men. Sergeants Laker and Riley were called over to Bartlett's tent. Lieutenant Bartlett greeted the two men, holding out two extra glasses he had managed to acquire along with a large bottle of Navy Rum, and this was a good excuse to explore the next day's training with his Sergeants over a warming drink.

"Gentlemen!" He always gave them the consideration of using the word 'gentlemen' instead of their surnames. "Tomorrow, after breakfast, we are to take our men down to the beach where the Pioneer Corps have built a replica pier or mole, sticking out into the Thames. We will be armed with rifles and machine guns, plus stun grenades, but obviously will only be using blanks. The idea is that two old Thames barges will pick us up, then make their way to the, er, mole. The barges will have ramps built into their sides; these will be lowered and our men must storm over and take the strong points on the mole. The defenders will have water canons, and will be firing with the intent of knocking us off and into the water; there will be swimmers to rescue anyone that does fall in; the idea is not seriously to drown our own, but a good fright won't do any harm. If, no, *when*, we capture their pennant, we must make it back to the barges and make our escape. Sounds easy, but somehow I think we are in for a shock!"

The next morning was very cold and wet; the men paraded in full kit and water just penetrated everything. Bartlett got them jogging around the field with the purpose of bringing warmth back to aching wet bodies. They marched down to the beach, which really was just some shingle mixed with copious amounts of mud. It stuck to everything and made walking in it almost impossible, but they had to comply, so they all found a way. They marched for about half a mile around the bay towards Eastchurch and there they found their barges! The shock of seeing these early nineteenth century vessels was intense; to a man they gaped in amazement. 'Was the hierarchy serious, did they actually have to get on board these frail craft?' 'One sneeze and we will all be dead.' 'Surely these were part of Noah's flotilla; they certainly are not safe for human cargo.'

'Christ, man, look at those ramps. They weigh so much that the barges are leaning over. This is all very suspect,' thought Lieutenant Bartlett. It was true: the extra weight of the steel ramps was making the barges lean quite heavily to the port side. He knew he must make his men stand evenly spaced aboard in order to stabilise the vessels, or this could all be a disaster in the making.

"Sergeant Laker, take half the men and place them on board that barge there," he ordered, pointing to the nearest. "Make sure that the men spread out quickly and carefully, making sure that the balance of the vessel is not compromised. We don't want any accidents, do we?" Laker didn't need to be told twice.

"Sergeant Riley, same goes for you on the other one. I am coming with you on that." Bartlett was shaking his head, and looked and felt extremely worried. 'Fancy giving us rubbish like this to work with. It shows scant regard for men's welfare and safety.' They were not exactly happy men.

The two barges lay heavily in the water; thankfully it was wet but not particularly rough; there was quite a heavy wind but it was coming from the South West, thus passing over the top of them. But Father Thames was receding, and the current was very strong; this again worried Bartlett.

"Pass the word, take great care not to fall in the river, one could get swept away. If you do have the misfortune to go for an early bath, scramble for a pier post, and wait to be rescued. Absolutely no heroics! Understood?"

Slowly the craft made its way upstream towards Minster and the mole that they had to take. Smoke was released from the beach; this was to fool the defenders, but since the tide was fast, as the smoke settled upon the water it quickly drifted away, so the men on the mole could see everything and everyone with no problem whatsoever.

Cautiously the two crafts tried to manoeuvre up against the dummy mole, but the tide made them crash against it with quite some force, enough to make the men spill to one side, thus making the tilt of the boat dangerous once again. Realising the danger involved, Bartlett screamed to all to move back so as to get the balance once more. But all the time the tide was making the barge crack against the mole. The pilot of the barge insisted that it was too dangerous: they would overturn and men would drown. But then, without thinking, he lowered the ramp, and as luck was most definitely on the side of the Marines, it came down, more or less on the mole. Nobody was going to miss this opportunity; up they went, over the top. Guns rattled, stun grenades were thrown, though where they were thrown, God only knew. Confusion reigned, hoses were turned on full power, and Bartlett watched in abject horror as his men got bowled over like so many ninepin skittles. Then he heard the splashes, and he knew that men were now in the river. 'This is not good,' he thought; then quickly made his way to the side of the craft he was in to see three men floundering quite badly. Two swimmers came alongside and quickly managed to rescue two of them, but as he watched he realised that Corporal Tillingham was the third man, and he was in serious trouble. Tillingham spluttered and gasped, he tried desperately to get hold of something, but the weight of his kit was pulling him down and under the pier. Bartlett watched, shaking with anger and help-lessness as he saw his trusted Corporal gradually sink beneath the water.

David, without fearing for his own safety, jumped straight into the brine, and kicked out to where Tillingham had disappeared: he knew that the weight of his kit would also stop him being swept too easily away. Bartlett took a deep breath, kicked his legs in the air and went under himself. It was cold and dark; the muddy water showed nothing at all to the Lieutenant, but he knew he must keep trying. A quick gulp of air, then under again. This time he would grope on the bottom and try and find his man. No luck again. Out of breath and feeling freezing cold and tired, he took one larger gulp of oxygen, kicked and went below once more. Third time lucky: he felt the webbing of his Corporal, grabbed it and kicked once again for the surface. When he broke into daylight, there were several swimmers around him, and between them they landed Bartlett and the very lucky

Tillingham. The Corporal was very close to death, and it did not help matters as when they tried to get him back onto the beach he hit his head quite heavily on a large piece of concrete. But he was alive, and he would recover, though the doctor might want to keep an eye on him for a day or two: after all, he had swallowed quite an amount of dirty Thames water, and with all the muck and filth that passed daily down the Thames, nobody wanted to be in the position of drinking it.

Much to the amazement of the now extremely cold and shivering Bartlett everything had gone quiet. All the Marines and the defending soldiers were looking over the edge of the mole, towards the luckless swimmers. Then it happened: at first it was just one man, then it was half a dozen, but soon it was everyone; clapping, cheering, throwing things around with wild joy to see their officer save one of them from drowning. How they all whooped with pleasure and Bartlett smiled a wry knowing smile! He knew what *he* was doing.

Though that first day's training had been a total failure, it did teach a salutary lesson. Never use poor equipment, realism was more important than just saving money and risking men's lives. The barges had been taken away, probably to the knacker's yard, though no one was told.

Men learnt to storm the pier, they devised means and ways. Soldiers learnt to trust their friends, but also to work for themselves. Bartlett was overjoyed at the way that things where progressing. Finally, a Thames ferry appeared, taken over by the Marines and Navy. This had its own ramp, and it was quickly put to use. They stormed the mole, three or even four times a day. Everyone now understood exactly what his role would be in the raid. Lieutenant Bartlett was aware that his objective was to take the mole at Zeebrugge, so every evening, time was employed to study precisely what their part would be with the help of maps and photographs; nothing was going to be left to chance.

For David Bartlett, these days had been the best of his life. He had loved every minute of it. He and his men had been given great praise by the other officers, and David had been singled out for being what he always wanted to be… a hero for saving Corporal Tillingham. But now the training was over; next would be the real thing. They would be presently sent back to Dover, along with the other units that were going to be involved. They could speak to no one, and they were all to be kept apart from any other parts of the army, until the day of the raid, especially with no contact with anyone from the outside world.

January turned into February; both months were cold and wet. Rough seas had been kind to British shipping, not allowing much U-boat activity. But March promised to be a smoother month. The weather forecasters predicted kinder times, less rain, less wind but still extremely cold weather. The fear was that March would once again bring the onslaught of the dreaded submarines and their torpedoes. Calmer seas would mean more shipping losses.

But there was one piece of joy for the British, as late 1917 brought the Americans into the conflict; with their extra ships surely the end was nigh for the Kaiser and his cronies? It was also true that armed raiders and better depth charges were now knocking out more U-boats than ever before. Things were beginning to even up as far as shipping losses were concerned. And in the war on the seas, because of the blockading, Britain was hungry, but Germany was starving. The Allies were most definitely outpacing the Central Powers.

VIII

It was Sir Roger Keyes who warned the war cabinet that Britain was not going to be in a position to carry the war to the enemy in 1918 and onwards, as the Hun was most definitely winning the battle of the Atlantic, Mediterranean and the North Sea. The Kaiser had bragged to foreign journalists that it took Britain three months to build a ship and the submariners three minutes to sink it. Keyes had taken this on board, and knew it to be true; if the British were expecting the war to continue into 1918 and onwards, then something had to be done about the U-boat threat. Maybe little could be done at this time in the Mediterranean, but the North Sea was different.

All the Allies had to do was block the two major ports of Ostend and Zeebrugge, thus blocking the way, either in or out, of U-boats and warships alike that took refuge within the safety of the ports; they would also not be able to use the canal leading to the comparative safety of Bruges. If these ports could be taken and blocked, the remaining U-boat force would have an extra six hundred mile journey around to the Baltic Sea, and that whole area was heavily patrolled by British warships as part of the on-going blockade of all German ports.

It was in 1917 that the then First Sea Lord, Sir John Jellicoe mooted the idea of the joint raids to the two Belgian ports. But Jellico's days were numbered as First Sea Lord, and it was not long before he was replaced by Sir Eric Geddes, mainly because he had shown great reluctance to implement the idea of ship convoys, which both Geddes and the Americans wanted, believing that many ships would be a greater deterrent to any passing U-boat. Jellicoe had always maintained that a convoy was only as fast as its slowest ship, which of course is true; this would give the submarines a chance to pick off many of the slower vessels, whereas single ships might just get lost in vast oceans. Both ideas had sound reasoning, but it was Geddes that won the day. Jellicoe was soon to become yesterday's man.

Keyes who had taken over as Admiral of the Dover Ports adopted the plans for the raid, and soon it was just a matter of crossing the '*t*'s and dotting the '*i*'s. Things were moving, and moving fast. It had been decided from the very beginning that the Royal Marines would have the honour of storming the two ports, but only extremely fit volunteers would be accepted. At Zeebrugge they would land against the mole there, which stretched almost a mile and a half into the sea, storming all the German strongholds and holding them against any counter-attacks that the Hun might try. Once the Marines were in place old block ships filled with concrete were to be sunk in mid-stream thus blocking the channels.

Soon that part of the plan was completed to everyone's satisfaction; they got their volunteers, and they were all capable men.

There were going to be seventy-five ships available for the raid, mainly old worn-out tubs such as aging destroyers, motor launches, monitors, and even two Mersey ferries. If they got sunk within the harbour area, they would themselves become part of the blockade. There were going to be two old British submarines, *C-1* and *C-3*, both filled to the gunnels with the high explosive ammonal; one was to be a suicide submarine, while the other was to be made available to rescue the volunteer crew of the first, unless for some reason, things went wrong, and then the second would be used as a mine as well.

The submarines were to ram themselves under the viaduct, and then the subsequent explosion would stop the defending German soldiers from re-attacking the areas that the Marines were to take, and hold. The remaining ships were to create as many problems for the Germans as possible, using smoke screens, heavy artillery, and even trying to shell another part of the area within a mile or two of the ports, with the hope that German re-enforcements would be duped into believing a landing was taking place. All very sound on paper, but would it work?

Sir Roger Keyes was a man who would get his own way no matter what; since his appointment, he had become completely single-minded about anything to do with the English Channel, and the sinking of the German U-boats. Keyes had decided to use the expertise of Wing Commander Brock, the fireworks king. Brock was to devise a new type of flare, so bright that nothing trying to run the Channel gauntlet would get through unseen. This was duly done; though the flare created a mild form of poisoning to the handler, it was thought to be a fair price to pay. On the night of the first use of the flare, a submarine was caught on the surface, and then sunk by the shore batteries, which Keyes had kept up to scratch by demanding that their aim be forever being refined. Within a very short space of time three other U-boats were sunk; having been caught in the dazzling light, they quickly submerged, only to hit underwater mines. So, in a matter of a couple of weeks, after the new flares had been brought into service, four German submarines had been summarily dispatched to the bottom.

The interesting aspect of this exercise is that the German authorities never knew why their U-boats did not make it back to base, and as long as that was the case, then the sinking could continue unabated. The fact was that most U-boat Captains and crew were desperate to try a Channel run, rather than go the safer route around the British Isles because it cost many hundreds of miles more, and extra days away from loved ones. Loneliness can and does bring on carelessness. As submariners were often on duty for several months at a time, when leave was due, the quickest route available became uppermost in their minds, and safety often went out of the turret.

Keyes was now onto a winner: there was nothing to stop him, yet there were still many high-powered Admirals and Captains who resented the way he had obtained his new exalted position. Another show of strength was needed; that came when he heard on the grapevine that three old German destroyers had been allowed to pass through the Channel, and while on their little excursion, they had managed to sink one trawler and seven drifters, who were there to help patrol the line for the Navy. They then shelled and badly damaged a paddle steamer and three more drifters, all this without a shot being fired in anger at them from the shore patrol or any British destroyers.

Keyes was completely unable to contain his rage when he heard the second-hand news. Heads must roll, and this was going to be the perfect excuse he needed to show he was in charge and that whatever anyone thought of him or his tactics, they would obey, and obey without questioning his authority. It was soon revealed that two British destroyers had been in the area, and when approaching the German ships, signalled them to stop, but as the three enemy destroyers didn't answer or communicate back in any way, it was thought they must be allies as the Hun would have opened fire or capitulated, so they were allowed to pass unhindered.

A court of inquiry agreed that the two Commanders of the ships *HMS Amazon*, and *HMS Termagant* should be severely reprimanded, which was really a slap on the wrist. Keyes was not having any of this as a punishment, and in the end both officers were dismissed from the Navy.

Keyes also wanted to punish a monitor Captain; *M26* had also been lying within the vicinity and had done nothing. He accused the Captain of outright cowardice when faced by the three Hun Destroyers, but the truth was he hadn't even seen them. Admiral Keyes was dissuaded from bringing any charges against the luckless Captain when he found out that the man had won a DSO when bravely fighting on a Q-ship against the U-boat scourge.

This was once more a test of strength, one that Keyes yet again won hands down. From now on, everyone would play the game according to the rules of Sir Roger Keyes, without any exceptions.

Now people would work, and work hard. Plans were well under way for the raid on Zeebrugge and Ostend. Nothing would stop it, even though time was running very quickly against them. How long had they to plan all this and bring the entire works together? No time at all: the raid was planned for 23rd April 1918, and already it was February 27th. But this was all done in the best British traditions of mismanagement, and that 'never say die attitude' that made Britain Great, a country where the sun never set on its Empire. This was going to be real 'Boys Own,' the stuff of legends.

IX

Christmas of 1917 came to Plymouth like in the rest of Britain, cold and wet. The sun was hardy ever to be seen, and the days dragged, leaving everyone feeling that something better should be happening in their lives. It is one thing to be continuously cold and wet, but another misery to add to lives already filled with woe when you went to work in the dark, and returned home with the same depressing outlook.

But for Harris this particular festive season had been happy and sad at the same time. The happiness came when his two sons, Michael and Andrew, who were on Dover patrol both managed to get home leave at the same time. The sadness came when their youngest son, James, now just eighteen, informed Steven and Barbara that on the 1st of January 1918, he would be travelling to London where he had enrolled in the Household Cavalry. His argument was that if he didn't join up, then in a short space of time he would be called up, as now conscription into the forces was being made compulsory.

Barbara was inconsolable, even when Steven pointed out how prophetic James's words were. But both parents felt great unease as the daily papers were showing just how many sons of Britain and its Empire were being slaughtered on the fields of mud and bullets. Steven and Barbara worried enough about the oldest sons, but thought that they were probably extremely lucky being on Dover patrols and not stuck at the front in France, Belgium or any other theatre of war, where men were being swatted like so many flies. Steven knew that James would be going to France just as soon as his training period was up, and the likelihood of him returning was just about even, the odds of him returning unscathed now most definitely against.

"Why didn't you join the Navy like your brothers?" enquired Steven with a deep frown showing on his forehead.

"Because, Dad, two is enough; I want to do my own thing. I will be alright, I can run faster than any bullets," he remarked whimsically, but nobody construed it as a joke.

"Well, your mother and I are not happy about this, but what is done is done. We cannot turn the clock back; if you have signed, you must now do your duty, and we will have to hope and pray that you are kept safe and sound, until this disastrous bloody war is over."

All in the house were more than a little shocked by their father's outburst: he never swore, at least never within the confines of the hearth and home. Barbara had even gone a slight shade of pink because of his cursing.

All in all, for the Harris family, Christmas had been a jolly time, putting aside the news from James. They dined well, as Steven had managed to pull in a few favours and acquired not just a huge goose, but a very large haunch of beef, plus two very large pike. They were not going to go hungry! The landlord of their local pub, *The Jolly Roger*, knew it was always a good time of the year to keep in with the Police, and as Harris was a Chief Inspector and a local man to boot, one might be inclined to allow a few bottles of port, wine and beer go extremely cheap in the direction of the Harris household, then maybe when hours went over, eyes would be averted. So the Harris family never went thirsty either.

Each meal had been a joy, each evening had been very good fun, when they played games, sat around the piano and sang songs from old and new times. They had attended church, where Steven was a Deacon, though why he was one, he really didn't understand, as he was more or less agnostic about God and the church. They went for long walks, across downs and along the beaches. They even went to the *Jolly Roger* to toast the landlord. But nothing lasts forever, and all too soon Christmas turned to be the New

Year. The older brothers left on the 30th of December, as they were expected back for duty the next day. James decided to leave at the same time, even though he would be turning up at the barracks at least one day early. He thought it prudent to get the goodbyes over in one go, not that Barbara or Steven agreed, but the lad was now nearing manhood, and he could come and go as he pleased. It was sad to say goodbye, all felt the torture that Barbara was going through, but all agreed that this holiday had been one of the best that they had had in years, one for the book of memories.

The three boys left, leaving a yawning chasm in the heart of Steven and Barbara. Neither of them slept well the first night without their lads, but as Steven had negotiated a decent break over the Christmas period, starting on the 22nd of December, and not returning back to work until the 2nd of January, he considered it prudent to stay at home with his wife until that date, even though he was refreshed and ready to return to the fray. But when the 2nd came, it was really a great relief to be seeing other familiar faces, and getting down to the nitty-gritty of human failings and wasted lives. 'After all,' he thought, 'this is what I know, and this is what I am good at!'

The first person he bumped into as he passed through the police station's doors was the exiting figure of his old friend Inspector John Cutler.

"Happy New Year, John! Did you have a good Christmas?"

"Happy New Year to you, Steven. Yes, I guess I did, but that now seems a long time ago. How are the family?"

"Good, it was special for the five of us to be at home at the same time. But one bit of not so good new is that James has joined up. The silly ass has enlisted with the Household Cavalry, he would have started yesterday. Barbara was beside herself when she received the news; but as he said to us, had he not enlisted, he would have been called up soon, anyway."

"Oh yes, conscription. I really don't know where I stand with that new law? With all the killing that is going on, there will be no youth left to repopulate this world after this fracas is at an end." Seeing that Steven was looking more than a little upset with the talk of killing off the youth, he decided on a different tack. "Steven, I am supposed to be visiting the morgue, but that can wait a few more minutes; let's have a cup of tea together, I wish to update you on our Cynthia murder."

Steven was taken aback, as he had given Cynthia a wide berth since they had been told to wait for letters to be sent to more powerful people who just might be able to unblock their way in the investigation. In fact both had not really done anything else, or given much thought to Cynthia, both being extremely busy clearing up past crimes, arresting criminals and generally trying to make Plymouth and the surrounding areas safer places to live. They both re-entered the station, making their way to Harris's office.

"Williams! Two teas, please, strong and sweet, and be quick about it!"

They sat down on the chairs around Steven's desk; Cutler leaned back, put his left hand under his chin and stroked an imaginary beard.

"One thing you don't know, in fact two things you don't know," spluttered John Cutler as, like many before him, he nearly fell backwards on his chair. "We heard from Edinburgh. They investigated the idea of Lady Jane being involved with an ornithological group, and guess what?"

But Harris was one jump ahead.

"Lady Jane did belong to such a group! And I bet a day's wage that they had another instrument maker as part of the group, but he isn't there now... Am I right?"

"One hundred percent right. What is more, we now have a real name, Deborah Winters. Sadly, her mother and father are both dead, and though she had a brother, he is in the army out in Mesopotania; he might well be dead for all we know. No one that knew Deborah has any idea where he really is or what he is doing, and once again getting anything out of the War Office is like getting blood out of a stone. Again, our man seems to have formed an attachment to Deborah, and when she disappeared, so did he. The thought generally was that they had left together, so that is why nobody really missed her." But then John dropped a bombshell. "We have got a very good description of our boy. He is extremely fit, over six feet tall, clean cut, always dressed as if going somewhere special; when he did go on field trips he would always wear a very neatly pressed pair of brown overalls. They were sure he was military, mainly because of his appearance, but he wouldn't reveal what he did to anyone, managing to avoid the truth when the question was asked; he went by the name of Roger Glencross. One other thing, and this you will like. He reminded them all of Douglas Fairbanks. He had a small neat moustache and a scar above one of his eyes, though nobody could remember which eye. Are we on to something, or what?"

"Fantastic news, bravo, John! You said you would never give up on poor Cynthia, and you haven't, nor have I," said Harris leaning forward onto his desk, with a gratified smile. "What was the second bit of news?"

"Ah, yes; we found out which group Cynthia belonged to, here in Plymouth, and sure enough our boy was there too."

"Well, have you taken this news to Chief Constable Jolly yet?"

"No, like you, he took a very long holiday, but he is back tomorrow, so maybe we can both go together and see what can be arranged and whether he has had any luck with his letters."

Both men were elated by the discovery of people that could actually identify their suspect. Subsequently, both enjoyed the rest of that day very much, yet did not give it much thought as to why they did. Cynthia Richmond had made an indelible impression on both their lives, and with the almost certain knowledge that their man was responsible for at least two other deaths in appalling circumstances, anything that could lift that burden upon their souls had to be an improvement.

Getting away from the case was probably the saving grace for both officers; they had for a while succeeded in forgetting the Richmond case, or at least almost managed it. But it always hung there, it was never going to go entirely away, even if they saw the perpetrator hang; somehow this was going to be their blight, one they would have to bear for life.

But today John Cutler's feet hardly touched the ground. He was off to the morgue to see an old friend for the last time, a man that had been the bane of his life for several years, getting away with the worst sort of crime, at least in Cutler's eyes, one of extortion. The man was Alfie Barnett; 'a nastier piece of work one would hope to meet,' was the thought running through Inspector Cutler's mind as he raised the shroud from over Barnett's body, looking down upon someone about whom he could easily say, 'it couldn't have happened to a more deserving person.'

Barnett had been a minor criminal in many ways, but made his living by putting the frighteners on people, mainly old lonely people. He would stalk a man or woman who might be living alone, until he knew their whole daily routine; once familiar with their habits, he knew just how they thought and managed each day. He would turn up at the person's door, forcing an entry, then intimidate that luckless being in such a way that they would always agree to pay a certain amount of money to him on a regular basis. He had got away with it because he would systematically use a little violence, never enough to seriously hurt, just sufficient to scare the life out of the victim. Sometimes things went wrong, and the victim would have a heart attack and die; Barnett always stayed, making sure the person had actually died, and then he would carefully ransack their abode, stealing whatever he thought would be valuable to him.

Everybody knew he did these things, but the police was never lucky enough to get a victim to talk, and Barnett was telling nobody anything, so over the years he had got more and more daring. He had taken to carrying a shotgun; at first it was not loaded, but recently he had shells up the twin barrels. If he got any difficulties from his 'paying public', then he would usually fire one shot into their ceiling, making sure that they understood that the next one was for them.

It had finally gone wrong for him: after stalking a lonely old farmer he turned up at his cottage at Lee Moor the night before last; while waiting for the farmer to answer the door, he stupidly placed the barrels onto the soft ground, and leaned quite heavily on the stock. When farmer Haydn opened the door, he was revealed as being a little younger than Barnett had presumed, but with the coercion of the gun he thought he could tackle him anyway. Demanding money, he pointed his shotgun up in the air, and when Haydn laughed in his face, he pulled the trigger. The old firearm blew up there and then. Alfie caught the full force of the exploding barrel in his face, and he fell to the ground in agony. At first farmer Haydn was shaken, but after recovering his senses, he then retrieved his bicycle; pedalling like mad to the nearest person he knew had a telephone, he called the police and the doctor. It was the doctor who arrived at his farm first. When the police finally made it Barnett was close to death; but the investigating officer was a very shrewd clever man, and he managed to convince the villain that his life could be saved if he made a full confession; which he did, and then promptly died.

Cutler replaced the sheet over Barnett's smashed face. He smiled to himself, and then went to the telephone to make sure that the local paper knew the complete inside story; this way any of the victims that the police didn't know about might be lucky enough to read about their forthcoming freedom from torment. 'A good day's work,' mused Inspector Cutler, and then left the building, thinking he would get back to the police station and get into some more work. But as he started to walk back to his work place, he saw across the road from the morgue the 'La Belle Tea House'; this was an establishment that had acquired a fine reputation for being able to serve good teas, coffee and cakes. Maybe he deserved treat instead of toil, which seemed a much better idea.

The 3rd of January came with rain, hail, strong freezing winds and general discomfort to all. Harris arrived at the station early, and for once he had put on his best pinstripe three-piece suit. He sported his grandfather's gold fob watch and chain, wore a wing collar shirt with a black matching tie. He was more suited for a funeral than a day's graft at Plymouth's main police station, but he felt that if he was to make some sort of impression on Chief Constable Jolly, he needed to look the part himself, and that meant dressing up. Jolly wasn't there when he first tried his office, so he waited for John Cutler to appear, then maybe have a cup of tea while sitting down formulating some sort of plan. Why he needed a plan of action he was not quite sure, but deep within the recesses of his mind, that was what spoke to him. Inspector Cutler looked at his old friend with almost disbelief, as he himself was in his usual rather worn-out attire.

"Has someone died in your family?" John Cutler queried with more than a little humour attached to his tone of voice.

"That is exactly what Barbara said as I left the house this morning. I don't know, I just felt that this was too important to be normal. I keep believing we need a coordinated plan of attack, but heaven knows *what* we have to attack. I guess Jolly will be amenable to whatever it is we have to do, but I can't help feeling apprehensive."

"Well, one thing we can do is not to wait until he gets into a negative frame of mind, but to hit him straight away with the new developments: our up-to-date news regarding the naming of Deborah Winters in Edinburgh, and the witnesses of our probable Royal Marines murderer. That will keep this case alive if nothing else will! But to be truthful, Steven, who in their right mind would stop the investigation knowing there is a homicidal murdering maniac on the loose?"

"Well, I still feel that dressing up was the right thing for me to do, even if it is the first time in years. Shows you how important I regard this case!"

After another three hours' wait, lots of tea drunk, the consuming of their sandwiches, and even the closure of several of their cases, at long last, in strolled a very late Chief Constable Jolly.

"Sir, have you got time to see Cutler and myself, it won't take long?"

"Always time for you two… Are you off to a funeral?" Jolly looked sideways at Steven Harris. "Have I forgotten something, or is this private?"

"Sir, I just felt the need to dress a little differently today. No funeral, at least I hope not."

"So, gentlemen, what can I do for you?"

Cutler jumped in before Steven could open his mouth again.

"Sir, we have some more very important new evidence in the Richmond case, which we want you to know about."

He then proceeded to explain all the new developments, bringing everything right up to-date.

"But, before we can interview any soldiers, we need that permission, and we were wondering if you had received anything or heard anything?"

"You are convinced in your own minds that we are looking for a Marine?"

"No question about it; we both feel one hundred percent certain that we are dealing with a member of the Royal Marines. Our man is in his late twenties, good looking, well groomed, with a scar above one of his eyes. One witness said he reminded him of the film actor Douglas Fairbanks. He is also interested in ornithology and can paint to a very reasonable standard. I think we are very close to nailing the swine." Steven looked at John to see if he was going to add any more, but he just smiled and nodded in agreement.

"Well, I have to tell you, I have received no letter of authority, only a letter to acknowledge my own correspondence. I think it is time to start writing more letters, and maybe using a subtle threat or two again, about possible newspaper coverage? Don't worry, I am not going to wind this down, we will get our man. I might even make a few telephone calls. It *will* happen. If you are not going to a funeral, Chief Inspector, I am very impressed; does this mean I can expect all my non-uniformed officers to come as neatly dressed as you?" With this he winked at John Cutler, who immediately turned bright red.

"Well, er, I er, oh dear! I must get on with my work."

John quickly followed Steven out of the smiling Jolly's office and back into his own den, sat down, drew two cigarettes from a packet, offered one to Harris and proceeded to light both of them.

"I am amazed, Steven: your dressing up brought the best out of Jolly, so it wasn't wasted. I have never seen or heard that man enjoy a joke, but he did today. Who knows, that might have swung it for us?"

"Don't be silly, he knew the importance of keeping the Richmond case open. But I have never seen him in such a jolly mood, excuse the pun. Well, yet again, it is now down to Chief Constable Jolly and his skill in letter writing."

"Williams! Two teas, please, sweet, strong and..."

"I know sir... hot! Coming right up."

"Just one thing, Steven."

"What's that, John?"

"Did you know you have egg stains down the front of your waistcoat?"

Chief Inspector Harris immediately looked down at his front.

"Oh, bloody hell!"

Many weeks went by, and so did the winter. Once again both Steven Harris and John Cutler got on with many other cases. The station was running like a well oiled machine. The clear up rate was exceptionally good, and many important cases were being put to bed for the last time, and numerous criminals were being sentenced and imprisoned.

News from the war came and went, leaving both the Inspectors sad about the casualties, but generally feeling detached from any of it.

Harris's sons, Michael and Andrew, were still busy doing their Dover patrols, while James was still undergoing training. It would be unlikely that James would leave for France before the end of March or even April.

The news had been encouraging on the Western front in the last few months, even being celebrated with the pealing of church bells when the whole country thought that there had been a major breakthrough at the tank battle at Cambrai in France, which started on the 20th of November 1917; there was a general belief that the tanks had punched a huge hole in the so-called impregnable Siegfried Line. Over four hundred iron monsters had crashed over the German trenches, killing many Germans as they lumbered, but the most important feature of the tanks was their ability to smash the German barbed wire. But like all the Allied attacks before, it was poorly organised, and the Cavalry, who were supposed to exploit the opening, failed to appear. So after a couple of days, instead of General Haig swapping jokes with the Kaiser in Berlin, the British were once again driven back to their starting position. But one thing was proven from this melee: tanks were the future; they were the lumbering beasts to break any deadlocks. Trench warfare would never be the same again.

Finally, on the 16th of April 1918, the authorisation came from the War Office that two Inspectors from the constabulary of Plymouth could, having been allowed to enter Dover Castle, interview any and all of Colonel Chartiers' small force of Royal Marines. This was the section of the Marines that had been in Edinburgh, Harwich and Plymouth at the time of the murders. What is more, the very day before, Cutler had received a telephone call from Police Constable Whitely to say that farmer Martyn Jones had been ploughing up the field opposite his home with his old horse and plough, and they had unearthed a brown set of overalls, which were quite undoubtedly covered in dried blood. This was good news indeed for Cutler and Harris: yet more ammunition to throw at the troops. It was now time to telephone through to Dover Castle and make an appointment to see Colonel Chartiers.

"Colonel Chartiers, this is Inspector Cutler, speaking to you from Plymouth. I understand that you have received a directive to allow us to come and interview your men concerning three murdered women. We would deem it a great favour if we could come more or less right away, as these hideous murders have gone unpunished long enough. I know we can rely on your complete cooperation." With this last sentence Cutler had his fingers crossed behind his back.

"Well, this is not at all convenient. We are just about to go into action, and I really do not want to disrupt my troops. This is a very important operation, one that is going to take a lot of men into great danger; many will probably not return."

"Nevertheless, Colonel, I really must insist that we are allowed to do our duty. We are trying to hold off the press, but unless I can give them some sort of story soon, they will draw their own conclusions, and that will be far worse than a couple of police officers interviewing your command, surely? Sir, they are well aware that these three terrible murders have been perpetrated, probably by a Marine; it will not take a hack writer long to start putting two and two together and make five. Please, sir, I beg you, let us drive down tomorrow and talk this through. We can be with you early on the morning of the 18th. "

Finally, and very reluctantly, Chartiers agreed. They could come, and they could do their interviewing.

X

Ever since Lieutenant Bartlett had received the news of the forthcoming attack on the mole at Zeebrugge harbour, he had been in a state of euphoria. He knew within himself that his entire life had been building up to this moment, and nothing was going to interfere with his plans, or those of his men. He had learnt that he and his unit of Marines were to spearhead the attack directly from a ship called *HMS Vindictive*. This ship was being fitted with ramps that would be lowered onto the mole so that the men could disembark quickly. Their task would be to take the enemy guns, prior to holding those positions until the various ships were sunk in the channels; then and only then could they think about a retreat. The ship was being padded with extra protective armour above and below the waterline. More guns were being added, and any superstructure that seemed superfluous to needs was dismantled. It was starting to look more like a floating tree house than a ship of the line. They were even placing old mattresses around the top deck, so as to slow any incoming fire, though how a straw filled mattress was going to stop a bullet was anyone's guess.

Training for Bartlett and his men was extremely laborious, and took up at least ten hours of every day. They practised landing and jumping on and off ships; men did get hurt in these exercises, but fortunately there were no fatalities. The nearest they got to a fatal accident was when Corporal Bolt who was a fresh recruit from Bartlett's unit, having climbed successfully onto the makeshift mole from the boat which represented the *Vindictive*, pulled the pin on a Mills bomb, and then dropped it before he could throw it. Bartlett saw this and immediately jumped into the crowd of men that surrounded the grenade, picked it up and threw it before anyone knew what was happening; it exploded harmlessly in the sea, off the port side of their boat. With that action, Bartlett saved several of his men, and they knew it. Corporal Bolt was beside himself with shame, but Bartlett patted him on the shoulder and quietly said, "Try not to do that again. It scared the pants off me, and I don't want to have to do any heroics again, I am getting far too old."

"Sorry, sir, it was plain clumsy of me; I really don't know what else I can say."

"Then don't say anything, and neither will I. Accidents can and do happen, but we must try and keep them to a minimum." Lieutenant Bartlett placed a hand upon Bolt's shoulder again, patted him gently, then moved away to get on with the training.

The men were now becoming very proficient, doing the exercising; the more they worked the quicker and better they got. But they all knew that the real thing would be different: there would be incoming fire from enemy guns. Men could and would be dying; everyone knew this was not going to be a pushover.

Every evening after work, there were lectures, which all the men had to attend. Soldiers had no leave, no chance to even go to the local pub; all taking part were confined to barracks. Even letters home were censored. Not even the officers were now allowed out, which meant that a lot of socialising went on in the various messes. Drinks were cheap and plentiful, a variety of games sprang up, causing all sorts of problems as all Royal Marines are competitive, and if a game was lost by someone too often, then that might induce a fight. And as now time was getting close to the off, fighting generated enormous complications when the Commanding officer had to bring to bear some sort of punishment. Generally punishment consisted of extra work instead of fun. Serious offenders might lose some days' pay as well; but nobody was given glasshouse duties as each man had a role to play and could now no longer be replaced with someone

109

else. The men quickly understood this, and problems started to get slightly out of hand, as the perpetrator knew he would more than probably just get a slap on the wrist, which really meant getting away with it. Lieutenant Bartlett also saw how quickly his men were abusing the system, so with the help of his trusted Sergeants, he gathered his entire unit together just before dinner was served.

"Men, I know you all well enough to talk to you on equal terms. We have all, or most of us anyway, been together since the start of this war in 1914. Each of us wanted and expected to get into action long before this; after all, isn't that why we joined the Royal Marines?" He slicked back his black hair, which for the first time was beginning to show just a hint of grey at the temples, and then continued. "You have all worked extremely hard over these last few weeks of training; I am very proud of you, and very happy to be leading you after such a long period of waiting. But, and I know the people involved know who they are, we have had a few problems with fighting. You must wait and fight the Hun, not one another. Anyway, it must stop now... and I do mean *now*. I have it on good authority that anybody else caught fighting will be thrown off the team, but that also includes the commanding officer, which in this unit, would be me. I, and all of you have worked too hard to lose our chances of going now. So, clean slates, no animosity between one another here or in other units. Heal any bad feelings that you might have towards one or two other persons. Learn to get on, carry on working hard, and let us all become heroes when we do our duty to God, King and Country. Now, get out of here, enjoy your meal; I guess you have all earned it, but no more trouble, or anyone caught will be handed to the Kaiser personally for punishment. Agreed?"

There came a roar of laughter and clapping, and in the general hubbub could be heard the reply... "Agreed, sir."

Sergeant Riley looked towards Sergeant Laker and winked. When they were alone together, Riley commented, "He is unbelievable, how he got those roughnecks to see his point of view. He certainly understands human psychology; at least I think so, as I am not quite sure I know what it means."

Both men laughed, and then followed their men into dinner.

Training went on unabated, muscles were finely tuned, brains knew and understood exactly what was expected of each individual. It had become just a wait until the time was called for the off. Any day now.

Bartlett had seen the letter from the War Office instructing Colonel Chartiers that he must allow the Plymouth police access to his men, and give all assistance. Bartlett knew that his days were almost certainly numbered; he would have to pay for what had happened, even though he never thought about his deeds or the consequences. He did not see himself as a maniac killer; he did not think he was insane. In fact after each killing had taken place, he did not think about it at all. That was for others to draw their own conclusions. He had done what he had to do, it had not been the voice of God or Satan telling him what to do, it had not been something that he had planned from early childhood, it was something that just happened, and it meant nothing, as swatting a fly on a hot summer's day means nothing. He was not stupid, he knew there was going to be trouble, but he did not give that a thought either. But as from now, it was all getting probably too close for comfort; he had to think how he could fulfil his destiny. How would he become that vaunted hero if the police finally got onto him? He would just have to stall things a while; once on the raid he would do what had to be done, nothing else mattered.

It was the evening of the 18th of April, training was over, and all the men were parading before being dismissed for the evening chow. Much to the surprise of everyone there, Colonel Chartiers came to the parade and asked to speak to all the men. To Bartlett's horror, he was not alone; with him were two civilians, who looked exactly like policemen.

"Tonight you will be taken from here to your boarding point, since this is the day that your raid is to take place. But before you depart, I have a very unpleasant task to perform. Beside me, as you can see, are two civilians;

111

both these men are Inspectors from the Plymouth constabulary, and they wish to look you over and ask you some questions. Do not be afraid, they have been here all day talking to the other units. You are the last batch. They wish to talk and ask about three very serious crimes that took place over the last year. Be honest and precise; I am quite sure that their facts are wrong, but we are obliged to help them with their investigation. Like I said before, I am quite sure that they are wasting their time, but let's make sure, eh?"

Bartlett went white as the Colonel spoke, but he wouldn't give himself away, not now they were so close to going. He called Sergeant Laker over, and asked him to get the men to drop their packs and equipment and make an orderly line. He then moved over to Chartiers and stood smartly to attention and saluted his Colonel.

"Sir, we are ready for the policemen to speak to the men. Do they want to do it here or in some other place?"

"No, here will be fine. The men are rightly hungry after all the work, so the sooner they do and say whatever these officers want, the better; let's get this nonsense over with as quickly as possible."

The journey from Plymouth to Dover had been an easy ride, only taking twelve hours with the careful driving of Constable Williams. But by the time they reached Dover all three were close to collapse, and in need of a serious night's sleep.

They retraced their steps and found the Inn that had housed them last time they were here. They dined well, and had a few drinks. But soon fatigue overtook all of them and they made their way to their bedrooms.

The next morning Inspector Cutler was up at the crack of dawn along with Constable Williams; they breakfasted quickly and were wondering when Chief Inspector Harris was going to appear when he came down the stairs to greet them.

"Jesus, Steven, you look awful, are you all right?"

"I think so; it must have been something we ate last night, but I have had indigestion all night long; the only relief comes from rubbing my chest."

"Well, what do you want to do? Do we stay here until you feel better or do we meet our ten o'clock appointment?"

"We go to the barracks, I will be alright, but I feel as if I need to burp all the time, yet I cannot burp easily. Strange, but never mind me, work calls."

Having not eaten or drunk anything Harris soon started to regret not taking a sandwich or even just a slice of bread. They reached the castle at a quarter to ten that morning. A guard yet again pointed a gun at them, while another went to see the duty officer.

"How you managed to get in to see Colonel Chartiers, I do not know. There is a war on, and usually it is quite impossible to get admittance. But there you go, things are changing all the time, and I have been told to take you both over to the Colonel's office where he will soon be able to see you." The duty officer bade them to follow, and they walked all the way from the castle entrance almost right into the old Norman keep, where the Royal Marines had their offices. They were taken into the rather cold austere office of Colonel Chartiers, but he wasn't there yet. The duty officer asked them to sit in the two chairs provided, and he stood back against the wall, where he could watch their every move. They waited, and waited. Eleven o'clock came and went; twelve o'clock came, only much more slowly. Harris was feeling terribly unwell, and he continuously rubbed his chest as the pain became more pronounced. He tried to get up and move around, but the duty officer warned him to sit still and wait. Cutler, in contrast, was starting to feel extremely annoyed at their lengthy wait, hoping upon hope that the Colonel was not doing this on purpose. At ten to one, in strolled Colonel Chartiers as if he had just been out to have a cigarette. There was no apology, no excuse, he just held out his hand to be shaken then sat down.

"So, gentlemen, what can the Royal Marines do for you?"

Harris was first to speak, and in a tone quivering with barely controlled anger, said, "Well, first, a hot cup of tea wouldn't go amiss."

The Colonel was at first taken aback, and then quickly regaining his composure, he asked the duty officer if he would be kind enough to do the honours. Soon, both police officers were feeling a great deal better and now ready to confront the Colonel with the questions that they had formulated in their minds.

"Colonel, first I want to start by saying that we are both very grateful for taking the trouble to see us. If you remember, I came to see you when you were encamped in Plymouth. I asked you if any of your men were out and about on the 21st of August 1917. You replied in the negative, stating that your men had been confined to barracks because of a fracas, so in your opinion no one had left the area. But we have conclusive proof that someone *had* been out and about." He was lying to Chartiers, but he needed to get him worried. "I will come straight to the point; we believe that one of your men has killed three women, slaughtering them in the most terrible fashion. One woman from Edinburgh has been decapitated, and her head and body cast into the sea, one from Harwich has been badly cut across her torso, and our own Cynthia Richmond was cut up from her navel to her neck. Now these murders were done in a very cold and calculating way, not for any sexual reason, but just what seems the joy of killing. We now know the sort of man we are looking for. He is at least six foot to six foot six inches in height. He has very neat jet black hair, and sports a small moustache, in fact he is a ringer for Douglas Fairbanks," at this Chartiers just looked blank, not knowing the name. "He also has a scar above his eye, but we don't know which one. He is also quite an authority on bird life, which is how he meets his victims; they all belonged to ornithological groups where there was a strong interest in the painting of the birds; we believe our man has that interest as well. Now surely that must bring someone to mind?"

"There is one other point that we would like to bring up." This time Inspector Cutler got out of his briefcase a rather dirty and bloody set of brown overalls. "Can you tell me if any of your men wear these sorts of overalls?"

"Er, yes, I do believe my men are allowed these when they are doing dirty work." He looked at the item of clothing closely, and then decided against actually picking it up. "Yes, these are without a doubt our overalls, but it wouldn't be hard for anyone to get hold of a few pairs. I see dockers and all sorts of people wearing them, probably sold to them by my Marines; you can't trust anyone these days."

The Colonel coughed, got up and walked around his desk to the window, from where he looked out onto the makeshift parade ground. He stroked his chin and his cheek and for a few seconds was lost in thought. The sound of Chief Inspector Harris vigorously rubbing his chest brought him back to reality.

"Well," stated Chartiers, "we have a big problem on our hands. What I tell you now must not leave this room, understood?" He stared at the policemen, waiting for their answer.

"Agreed, whatever you tell us that is not part of our investigations will not be revealed." But both Cutler and Harris had their fingers crossed behind their backs when they agreed.

"Right, well, the situation is like this. I can help you with most of my men, and we can have that taken care of more or less right away. But if that doesn't bring any results, then we have a problem, as roughly one hundred and twelve men and NCOs, plus one Lieutenant are involved with a raid that is going to be taking place within the next few days; those men will leave for the port tonight after their last day of training is over. This will give you precious little time to get organised and interview each man. But of course I want to help because of the story you have told me, though I don't believe for an instant that any of my Royal Marines are capable of doing anything as appalling as what you have described."

Colonel Chartiers told his duty officer to immediately muster on the parade ground all the remaining Marines under his control.

Then ensued a great deal of running to and fro, and within five minutes the duty officer reported that all the Privates and NCOs were now outside, ready to be questioned.

"Before we go out there, Colonel, can you tell me if you have lost any men since Plymouth, or if any have been transferred?" Harris once again rubbed his chest after finishing speaking.

"I will have to check that out; I really don't know if anyone has died or been transferred." Chartiers looked towards his duty officer, and then added, "Lieutenant Cooper, can you check that out for me, as quickly as possible, please."

The Colonel, accompanied by the two civilian police officers, walked out onto the parade ground. You could have heard a pin drop, if it hadn't been for the squalling of seagulls overhead. It was the noise from these birds that made Cutler look upwards and onto the roofs. He noted that everything was covered with bird droppings which surprised him for a second, knowing how fastidiously clean the army was. The Sergeant Major barked the command —"'Shun!'", thus bringing his attention back to earth, making him forget all about cleaning problems and concentrate about the task in hand.

"How do you want to handle this?" enquired Chartiers, looking towards the two police officers; his brow had deep frown marks extending down to his eyes.

"We would like to firstly go down the line of men and look for obvious points that might lead us to our man. Then it is a matter of interviewing each one in the privacy of an office, if that could be kindly arranged?" Cutler turned to Harris, "Can you think of anything else?" But a shake of the head gave the answer.

As each soldier stood erect at attention, eyes firmly facing front, it was easy for Cutler and Harris to slowly walk down the line, scrutinising each soldier in turn. They were looking for men matching the descriptions given. While they were engaged in doing this, Lieutenant Cooper appeared with the answer to their query. Only one soldier had died in the last year, having contracted influenza; several others had caught the virus, but he was the only fatality. The only person to leave the Marines was a very old Sergeant who had finally been pensioned off, and was now living in Leeds with his wife. Neither of these two people matched the description of the suspect.

It took approximately twenty minutes to check the entire assembly of men; much to the frustration of Cutler and Harris, not one came even close to match their suspect. A smile appeared on Chartiers' mouth, and he felt a certain smugness in feeling the expression, '*I told you so,*' come to his thoughts. Colonel Chartiers looked at Harris, and asked in a more gentle tone of voice, "Are you alright, Chief Inspector, you look extremely pale?"

"I have been suffering from something I ate last night, terrible indigestion, but nothing I do can shift it at the moment. It will pass, given time. Thanks for asking. If possible, can we have an office where we can do our interviewing?"

"Yes, of course. Lieutenant Cooper, can you arrange that immediately, please?" Then turning to his men who were still standing at attention, he said in a very deep loud voice that carried across the parade ground and up into the air, competing with the gulls for attention:

"Men, these two policemen are looking for someone who they think will turn out to be a member of our force. I think they are mistaken, but we must give them every assistance; that is why they went up and down each line of you. They are now going to interview each and every one of you. Help them with clear honest answers to their questions." He then promptly turned and walked back to his office. Once he disappeared inside a Sergeant barked out the command... "*Stand at ease!*" Within the next ten minutes the policemen had their private office, and had each soldier in turn come into it, sit down and answer the following questions.

"Has anyone you know ever sported a moustache, does anyone you know have a scar over an eye, does anyone you know paint bird life, does anyone you know ever joined an ornithological group, does anyone you know sport very sharp implements such as swords etc.," which always got the answer of: "we all carry bayonets."

One or two answers had been helpful, but were not really leading anywhere; there seemed to be no one that matched that description. The day went slowly by, but the two investigators managed to interview all the men; it was now getting dark, and the last group of soldiers would soon be finishing their training period; they would be the last of the interviewees, which left Cutler and Harris feeling very downcast, as nothing new had really come to light from any of the men. Both the Inspectors were beginning to have a hunch that this journey was not going to be the success that they had hoped for. Harris was starting to seriously doubt that the Marines were involved, but that a very clever psychopath was leading them a merry dance. His chest hurt more than ever; he was feeling dreadful, and he was cold and hungry as well. Cutler looked at his friend and began to worry about him.

"Steven, let's get this over with, and then I will buy you a fine meal, and get you back to the hotel for a good night's sleep. You look as if you need another holiday."

"I do feel awful, I cannot get rid of this ache in my chest. I also feel bloody depressed that this whole fiasco seems to be tumbling down around us; I am now having doubts as to whether it is the army or somebody else. I know this though: if we go back with negative replies to Jolly's questions, he will more or less close the case down." He sighed, looked at his friend, and then added, "Just another hundred or so men, then it's back to face the music."

Colonel Chartiers had walked back onto the parade ground to meet them.

"I will personally take you to meet the boys that are going on the raid. Please be gentle with them, they have all worked hard and are deserving of our respect for what they are about to do."

When the three of them walked over to the Roman lighthouse where Lieutenant Bartlett was parading his men, Bartlett looked surprised and confused. He stood back while Chartiers spoke to his men and waited until the two policemen were walking the line; he then went over to his Colonel to ask what this was all about. He knew what the answer was, but listened

118

intently anyway. Before the two policemen came back, he had slunk away from all of them with the excuse of a toilet trip. It took another two hours before Cutler and Harris admitted defeat, much to the amusement of Chartiers.

"Never mind, gentlemen, please come and dine with me before you leave; you can give me all the grisly details."

Harris would have preferred to go straight back to the hotel, but Cutler thought a good meal might just be the ticket for his friend.

As the three of them walked over towards the officers' mess, several lorries were loading up with Bartlett and his men, ready for the short trip to the dockyards and the ships. They were on their way! Lieutenant David Bartlett knew that nothing or anyone could now stop him; he was washed, packed, and ready to board the *HMS Vindictive*, next stop, Zeebrugge! His war was about to start!

"So tell me," said Colonel Chartiers to his two guests, "what is so special about this man of yours? What made you think that he might be one of mine?"

The meal was a fine roast of lamb, with roast potatoes and four different vegetables, which for both policemen were almost impossible to buy because of shortages within the country as a whole.

"Colonel, I must admit to being very confused. I was totally ready to believe that one of your men had been the killer, mainly because of the fact that each woman that died, died when you were camping close by. And also, the fact that all the people belonging to the bird watching groups think he was army. A very smart man, with dark hair, a scar over his eye, at least six foot tall, extremely strong, with a liking for blades or swords, loves birdlife and probably paints, mainly birds, at a guess. But we have interviewed all your men and there is no one that matches that description. We looked for that scar; many men did carry scars, but none above their eyes. I am beginning to think we got it completely wrong." Cutler then glanced at his friend who was looking more ashen than ever. "Steven, are you sure you are well? They have doctors here at the camp; surely we can find someone to have a look at you?"

"No, I will be alright. It is indigestion, I know it is."

An officer on their immediate left, who had been listening intently to their conversation, spoke, addressing himself to Colonel Chartiers.

"Sir, there is one man that loves to paint, and I know he is into ornithology."

"Oh, Captain Chambers, and who is that?" asked Chartiers with a totally indifferent, matter-of-fact tone of voice.

"Why, that is Lieutenant Bartlett, sir."

"Are you mad, Chambers? Bartlett is the salt of the earth; anyway, he is now aboard his ship and waiting for the order to up anchor. Officers don't do what this murderer has done; it is entirely out of the question."

"Sir," said Cutler to the Colonel. "We never did interview any officers; in fact, none came forward to be interviewed. Why was that?"

"I told you, no officer would do such a thing."

Cutler was not satisfied with this answer, and went for the jugular. "Sir, do you mean to tell me officers don't kill people in battle, and if they do, what is the difference between plunging a bayonet into some other soldier, and slicing up a woman?"

"Nonsense, man! An officer kills only because he has to, he would never kill for the sake of killing. I know all my officers, know them personally; I would know if they have the sort of problems that would perpetrate the sort of terrible things you have described."

"Well, as you know your men so well, answer me this question; Bartlett, Lieutenant you say; what does he look like? Can you describe him to me, please?"

"Of course I can. He is quite tall, maybe six foot six, he has black hair, always neatly combed."

"Does he sport a moustache, sir?"

Chartiers paused for a moment, tugged the lobe of his left ear and reddened before answering this last question.

"Why, yes, I do believe he does."

"And does Lieutenant Bartlett have a scar above an eye?"

"I don't think so." With this he felt a little more relaxed, or at least until Captain Chambers broke into the conversation once more.

"He does, sir; a small scar above his eye, I think his left one."

"Sir, in Plymouth, you informed Chief Inspector Harris that no one had left the post that day of the murder; did you mean *everyone* or could that just mean Privates? Could an officer have slipped through the net?"

Colonel Chartiers was starting to sweat profusely, and was now very reluctant to answer any more questions, as they would almost certainly bring trouble for him if there was to be a board of enquiry.

"Sir, don't you think it is time to get someone out to the ship and bring him back for questioning?"

"Sorry, Inspector Cutler, but that is now not an option: he is part of a mission that as from tonight has started. If Bartlett turns out to be your man, then you can only have him when and if he returns. He is a very important part of this operation; I cannot or will not jeopardise any element of this, even if he had killed the King himself. Is that understood?"

"Well, I understand only too well; but I think we should at least look at his room, if only to make sure that he is not the murdering swine? Does he possess a batman?"

"We can find out quite easily; Captain Chambers, find out who his man is, and if he is around or gone with him." He snarled out this last sentence, as he felt annoyed that this had all come to light because of the casual remark that Chambers had uttered. 'Why didn't the fool keep his big mouth shut?'

Five minutes later, in walked Chambers with a bald, rather rotund Private, who answered to the name of Joseph Smith. At that, all the conversations in the mess stopped, and everybody's attention concentrated on the small group.

"Smith, you know Lieutenant Bartlett well, I would think?"

enquired Cutler.

"Well, yes, sir; I know Lieutenant Bartlett very well. I wanted to go with them, but he told me I was too old and anyway, I had a wife and children and he felt it would be putting me in unnecessary danger. He is a kind and good man, sir."

"Yes, I am sure he is. Tell me this: did he go out of the barracks in Plymouth when all the men were confined to quarters?" Before Smith could answer, a groan came from Harris, which made everybody start. He was rubbing his chest vigorously, and was showing obvious signs of severe pain. It was Chartiers who first reacted.

"Chambers, get the MO immediately."

"Don't worry it is just... Oh!" Harris fell forward clutching his chest, his head hitting a plate and cutlery in the process.

"Steven! What is happening to you?"

"I would say your friend is having a heart attack, and a very severe one at that," interjected Chartiers, but with a certain amount of sympathy tucked neatly into his voice.

The doctor duly arrived, felt Harris's pulse, and then listened to his heart.

"Get a stretcher and quick, this man is close to death! He has had a heart attack, and he needs immediate medical attention which I can give him at the hospital block. Quick, man, time is important."

A stretcher was brought and Harris was quickly transferred to a bed of the hospital block, which fortunately was very close by.

This incident, and what had preceded it, had entirely ruined dinner: no one was in a mood to eat. All the time that this was happening, Private Smith stood silently to attention, awaiting some sort of order. It came from Inspector Cutler.

"Private Smith, do you have keys to enter Lieutenant Bartlett's room?"

"Yes, sir, I do."

"Well, man, I want you to take me there and show me around."

Private Smith looked dumbfounded, looking for support from his superiors. There was a shrug from Chartiers, which said it all. Smith must allow entry to Cutler into Bartlett's private quarters. Cutler was not going to be the only intruder: Chartiers followed, as did Chambers and three other officers who had all been quietly eavesdropping to the entire conversation from the moment that Cutler had asked the questions of who, how and why.

Lieutenant Bartlett had a small room, no bigger than twelve feet by fourteen. There was an iron-sprung bed very neatly made, in typical army fashion. A window looked directly out onto the dustbins, behind one of the cookhouses; what could a lowly Lieutenant expect? Opposite was a desk, with many papers very neatly stacked. When Cutler looked at them he knew he finally had his man. These were all drawings of bird life, and when looking closely at one of them he recognised that the drawing had been done from the hideaway that Wendy Bryant had been found dead in. There, against the far wall was the prize: it was a chest, and Inspector Cutler just had to look inside.

"Smith, do you have any keys for the chest?"

"No, sir; that is Lieutenant Bartlett's private chest, not for you or me to be looking into!"

Inspector Cutler looked directly at Colonel Chartiers; he now needed the permission from the reluctant Colonel, whose world had now been completely turned upside down.

"Are you sure this is your man?"

"One hundred percent, sir; the drawings now prove it to me."

"Smith, break it open, and try not to make too much of a mess."

Private Smith was completely baffled as to why all these officers and a civilian police officer would want to open a private chest for. But an order from a superior officer is an order that must be obeyed. He looked around for a hammer or tool that could break the padlock; there was nothing. He kicked it as hard as possible; not even a dent. He then asked to be excused while he went to the cookhouse to see if they had something that could be used as a lever. He came back with a claw hammer, though what the cook used a claw hammer for, one could only surmise! After pulling hard at the lock, managing to damage some of the exterior of the chest in his efforts, he finally managed to prise it away. Cutler looked at the Colonel who, from his facial expression, made it clear that he wanted no part in the opening of the lid: this job was up to the police. After all, hadn't he been ordered to cooperate fully? He didn't like it, but that was what he was doing. Cutler moved forward, removed the padlock and pulled back the broken lock. Raising the lid, for all to see, was Bartlett's 'Katana' Samurai sword with the 'Shoto' dagger that accompanied it mounted on a special stand. Cutler smiled, looked at Chartiers. As he lifted the sword from the chest; he made to pick it up. Having done this badly, the blade drew blood from his finger by merely touching it. He recoiled, this time with blood dripping from a small slit on his right index finger. Cutler continued and lifted the sword out of its stand so that all assembled could see what had been the killer's weapon. Turning to Colonel Chartiers, Cutler said:

"No officer could kill, eh?" — tables now completely turned.

"Inspector Cutler, one must have faith, or what the hell is life all about? But sometimes we get it wrong; does that make us fools, or just human?"

"Colonel, I would like your permission to have this room sealed until I can do a thorough examination."

"I will see to that immediately, Inspector."

At that the doctor came striding through the door.

"I have bad news, Inspector Cutler: your friend, Chief Inspector Harris died a few minutes ago; there was nothing we could do for him; he obviously suffered a massive heart attack. I am very sorry."

"Oh, Christ, this is going to be hard to break the news. Colonel, can I bring Constable Williams into the barracks? He has been waiting all day for us in the car at the main entrance, and if possible, could we stay the night here, and then make some calls tomorrow about what to do next?"

"Captain Chambers, please see to these requests." Chartiers looked down at his feet, and then added: "I guess you can stay, and I am thinking that you won't want to leave until the fleet come back from the raid. Right?"

"Right, Colonel, and thanks."

"Constable Williams, you have been exceedingly patient; having to linger around the entrance cannot have been any fun. Things have happened and we are going to be staying here for a day or two. I have some extremely bad news to convey to you, and telling you is easier than the next people I have to tell."

"What is it, sir, what has happened?"

"I am sorry to inform you that Chief Inspector Harris died about thirty minutes ago. It seems he had a massive heart attack over dinner; he just fell over at the table. I suspect he didn't feel a thing."

"Oh, sir, that is terrible. Have you informed his family yet? What about the station, have you telephoned back to them?"

"Not yet, Williams, but I suppose I ought to at least telephone the Chief Constable; maybe he can inform Harris's wife of the tragedy. Christ, man, I feel awful; yet on the bright side, if there is one, we have found our man. Not a Private like we thought, but an officer, with the name of Lieutenant David Bartlett; but buggeration upon buggeration, he is now on a mission and we can only get him if and when it is over, and he returns to Dover. It is a long story, but over a beer I will fill you in on the details."

The telephone call to Plymouth police station was difficult, not because of the tragedy, but because the line was terrible and Cutler could hardly hear anything said from the other end.

"I said this is Inspector Cutler speaking; *Cutler, Cutler*, man!" He was shouting so loud that he nearly did not need the phone: they probably just could have done with sticking their heads out of the window. "For crying out loud, doesn't anybody understand what I am trying to say?" His patience was wearing very thin; all he could hear was a mumbling voice, speaking in Mongolian for all he knew. He hadn't understood anything, but more to the point, Plymouth hadn't understood anything either. Eventually, a sympathetic Scottish woman's voice with a broad Glaswegian accent said,

"Inspector Cutler, it would be better if you tried again, maybe tomorrow morning. I am terribly sorry to say that there are very many technical difficulties showing up on the line to Cornwall, and hopefully they can be remedied by tomorrow."

"Look, operator, this is a very important police matter; I want to book this call for nine thirty tomorrow morning; it must get through. Understood?"

"Of course, sir, we will do our very best. We really are sorry for your trouble."

John Cutler didn't wait to hear any more, and hung up the receiver there and then. The look of frustration that Constable Williams could recognise on his face was one that was only going to pass after several large glasses of beer.

The next morning both police officers were awakened by the shrill trumpet sound of reveille, a sound that brought back memories of their time in the army. Alcohol had been the saving grace for Cutler: after his fourth pint of bitter, he had been ready for sleep; even the passing of his friend Harris now would not stop him falling into an unconscious dreamless state.

He rubbed his eyes and saw that the time was just six o'clock in the morning; he licked his dry lips, then realised that his head was not quite resting on his shoulders; at least it could not be, as it throbbed mercilessly. It was just becoming light, and the glare of what could be taken for a sun was just starting to move the sea mist which swirled around the castle and its grounds. Finally John Cutler roused himself, firstly to find a handy toilet, then to wash, shave and generally tidy himself up; he knew he represented the civil police, but that was never an excuse for not being neat and tidy and the same applied to Williams. When the two men met for breakfast, which to their delight consisted of eggs, bacon and all the trimmings that were becoming scarce outside of army life, they looked at one another, and agreed that drinking may help your sleep mode, but it does nothing for rousing yourself the next morning.

"Sir, how are you this morning?" but before he could answer,

Williams quickly followed on with, "I feel bloody awful; I really hope I have no driving to do today. I would just like to stay in bed and in the dark."

"Oh, come on, Williams, you are a young man! If you were in the army you would probably be drinking like that every day. Anyway, after yesterday, we both needed a boost, and the booze gave that to us."

"I suppose you are right; anyway, I always feel much better after a fry-up. But I can't help thinking about Chief Inspector Harris. Have you seen him yet?"

"No, I haven't, but we can do that after we have received our call at nine thirty."

It had been agreed by Colonel Chartiers that both officers could stay, just in case the mission to block Ostend and Zeebrugge was to be cancelled; if so, they could take Lieutenant David Bartlett into custody for questioning. But they had both been bluntly warned that they must not get in the way of whatever was going on; moreover they must not tell anyone why they were there, and not ask any more questions of anyone, unless they had been authorised by Colonel Chartiers first. They had been advised to use the officers' mess, it being thought that officers were less likely to ask questions or gossip. Many ranks came, ate and went, all the time avoiding the two policemen as if they had the plague. Time hung heavy, and it seemed like an age before Cutler turned to Williams and said:

"It is a quarter past nine. Let's walk across to the Colonel's office and await our call to Plymouth."

Nine thirty came, and the ring tone pealed out. The Corporal manning the telephone spoke into the receiver, looked up in the direction of Inspector Cutler, then gestured for him to come over and take the call.

"Hello, is that Plymouth police station? This is Inspector Cutler talking; can you connect me with Chief Constable Jolly, it is urgent!"

"Jolly speaking!"

"Sir, this is Cutler here; I have some extremely bad news for you. Chief Inspector Harris died last night of a massive heart attack; I tried to contact you yesterday but there were problems with the line. Could you convey the news to his wife for me, please? I really don't know what to say or do about him. I thought, with your permission, that I could contact a funeral director here in Dover and get them to make arrangements to have him taken home. Is that what you want me to do, sir?"

"Oh, no, good God! I thought he had been acting oddly over the last few months. Heart attack, you say? Yes, have him brought home. When are you coming back? And what about the killer?"

"Sir, good news and bad news on that front. Yes, we have our man, or at least we are ninety-nine per cent certain who it is." Cutler cupped his hand over the receiver so that no prying ears could overhear what he was saying to the Chief. "His name is Lieutenant David Bartlett; I am sure you are as surprised as we were when we found out it was an officer, and not a Private as we all assumed. But we cannot take him into custody, as he and hundreds of other soldiers are on a mission, and I'm not at liberty to talk about it. If, for any reason it all goes belly up, I have been assured by Colonel Chartiers that we can have our man. But as he is a very important part of whatever it is they are doing, we have to wait until they return which anyway will only be a day and a bit after the mission starts; of course he may be killed, wounded or captured; well then, what can we do? Nothing! Anyway, I have been given permission to stay and wait, and if you agree, what are another few days extra to close the Richmond case?"

"John!" This was the first time Jolly had called Inspector Cutler by his Christian name. "All this has been thrown at me on the sudden side. Make the appropriate arrangements for Steven Harris. In the meantime I will, and I hate this job, contact Barbara and let her know the sad news. Keep one eye on the Colonel - I don't trust the man for a minute – and make sure that this man of yours, er… Bartlett does not slip the net. I will also make certain that the War Office knows of your suspicions concerning him. If he can be taken now, all's the better, but if we have to wait until his return, then as you say, what are a few more days? This is a hard time for you, John, and I want you to know that we here at Plymouth appreciate all that you are doing, so keep up the good work. One last thing, keep in touch with me on a daily basis; nine o'clock is a good time as I shall be in the office. Is there anything else?"

"No, Chief Constable, and thank you for your support, it is much appreciated. I will be telephoning you tomorrow at the same time."

Cutler and Williams knew that it was now their awful duty to inspect the body of their friend and colleague. The makeshift morgue was a very dreary, solidly built room, which had been constructed for the storage of munitions; it was an extremely cold place, ideal for the storing of explosives like gunpowder. There, laid out on a trestle table with just a white sheet covering him was Cutler's old friend, Chief Inspector Harris. John felt the bitter taste of bile rise into his throat, but he managed to suppress it before it became obvious to Williams. But he could not stop the flow of tears from his eyes, as they ran down his cheeks and onto his jacket.

'Poor old Steven, and so close to his retirement. Christ, I hope the force will do the right thing by him, if not for him, then for his wife Barbara.'

Both Williams and Cutler moved over and looked closely at the body. Steven Harris was cold and stiff; he had turned slightly blue, which in itself took away any resemblance to the man they both knew. His face looked swollen and it had sunk into itself just a fraction, not enough to disguise who it was, but enough to confuse that feeling of recognition. In some ways Harris now looked just like any other dead body, and not like anyone that Cutler or others knew well; somehow that helped the Inspector to come to terms with what had happened a little more easily.

From the morgue they went to see the doctor who had pronounced him dead. He announced that there would have to be an autopsy, but to him it was an open and shut case, so he would perform that task himself, making it as quick and trouble-free as possible. All the paperwork could be cleared and the body made ready for the journey back to Cornwall by late this afternoon, if they so desired. As the army doctor could and would issue a death certificate, it seemed the best thing to do. Cutler would now go into town and make the arrangements with the local undertaker. They went back to the Colonel's office, firstly to get passes organised, mainly so they could come and go as they wished into the barracks, secondly to tell the Colonel what their plans were for the day, and where they could be found if any emergency occurred.

The day was well spent by Cutler and Williams; they made arrangements for the hearse to come to the barracks to pick up Steven Harris the very next day which was the 20th of April. They drove around the town to view as much of it as they could; there were many restrictions as to where they could and could not go: road blocks seemed to be everywhere. So eventually it was decided that a trip to Deal and Walmer might be in order; both these small towns were completely taken over by the military, but they managed at least to drive past both the Cinque Port Castles. The weather had cleared somewhat, and showed all the promise of being a nice sunny day, at least while you sat in a car, away from the wind that was churning the sea quite ferociously! Even in the sheltered areas of Deal the waves were breaking over the shingles at over six feet in height. The wind was cold, and was coming from the north-west. But while the two of them sat in their police car, it was reasonably comfortable. Yet again, there were road blocks everywhere, and being a police officer made no difference; no entry meant just that, no entry. It was just before five thirty that afternoon that Cutler remarked on how hungry he felt, so it was decided to make tracks back to the Castle and some decent free army food.

When they arrived at the main entrance, the duty sentry informed them that they must report immediately to Colonel Chartiers' office, as there had been some developments. Parking the car they almost ran into the office.

"We have been waiting for you. The doctor told me to tell you that the body of your friend is now cleared, and I have the death certificate here." Corporal Glasper handed a brown envelope to John Cutler. "I also have the telephone number of a Barbara Harris; she has asked if you would telephone just as soon as you come back here." Again he handed over a piece of paper with a few numbers written on it. "And finally, the Colonel has asked to tell you that if you wish to dine with the officers, dinner will be served precisely at seven o'clock, and would you both be kind enough to dress appropriately for the occasion?"

'Pompous old fool,' though Cutler, but he kept it to himself.

"Corporal, could you get me this number, please." He waited not more than three minutes before once again he was handed the receiver.

"Hello, Barbara, how are you feeling? The shock must be awful for you, as it was for us here. I had no idea that he was so ill. I am most terribly sorry!"

"Thank you, John, I know if there was anything that could have been done, you would have done it. John, I want you to do me a favour: can you contact our two oldest sons Michael and Andrew? I have no idea how you can do it, but they are based there in Dover, and both have their own torpedo boats. Maybe someone at the barracks will have some connection that you can use. Tell them everything, please, and ask them to contact me; if possible I will ask them to get special leave, or I shall postpone any funeral arrangements until they can make it back down here. Please, John, I know you must be busy, but unless I write letters to them both, and who knows how long letters might take to reach them, I have no other way of contacting them other than through you; can you try and help?"

"Of course, Barbara, I will make some enquiries and do what I can. In the meantime, Steven should be taken from here tomorrow; he will be delivered to the Plymouth police station within a day or two. Chief Constable Jolly will contact you to make all the necessary arrangements. If there is nothing else, Barbara, I will wish you well, try and sleep; one thing you should know, I was there when it happened, and he didn't feel a thing, he just fell forward and it was over." He heard the gentle sound of Barbara crying on the other end of the line, and he knew it was time to hang up the receiver.

The next morning, now getting used to the iron-framed narrow beds, they both arose to the sound of the trumpeter who somehow managed to make the gulls sound like a heavenly choir. After a very leisurely breakfast of two eggs and many slices of toast, and several hot cups of strong sweet tea,

Cutler managed to purloin a daily paper. Reading of the war efforts made him wince visibly.

"What is the matter, sir, you look as if you have seen a ghost in the paper?"

"Williams, be happy that you are in the police force and not over in France doing your bit for King and Country. The Germans have obviously brought the remaining troops from the old Eastern front to now play on the Western one. There are many battles going on all over the Champagne region, and many of the old Somme battlefields that we managed to capture in 1916 have now fallen again to them. Things are looking very bad for the Allies; thank God the Americans have joined the fun. God, let us hope there is enough time for the Doughboys to make a difference. Where does the Kaiser get all these extra troops from? Interestingly though, the paper says that most of the prisoners that we take are mere children. Anyway, we must find Andrew and Michael Harris and tell them what has happened."

It took just one telephone call from Corporal Glasper who was once again manning the telephones in Chartiers' office, to find the whereabouts of both men, and how to contact them. The second call was directly to Michael in the main dock at Dover.

"Michael, my name is Inspector Cutler; I worked with your father. I am afraid I have some very bad news for you: your father died two days ago here in Dover Castle; his body is being taken back to Plymouth, hopefully this very morning. If it is possible, can you and your brother get a couple of hours off to meet me as I would like to tell you the entire story?"

Cutler took a deep breath, and waited for the reply. Michael was quite composed and sounded very matter-of-fact.

"I remember dad talking about you at home. I will contact Andrew, that shouldn't prove to be difficult as both our Patrol boats are being prepared for a small excursion we have to make. Let us say we meet at, er... twelve thirty, at the *King Arthur*, in Hope Street. Would that suit you, Inspector? In the meantime I shall contact mum. Thanks for letting me know."

At nine o'clock precisely Cutler telephoned Jolly, giving him the update on what was going on. The Chief Constable agreed that bringing the body to the police station would be fitting before taking it to the local Chapel of Rest: that way all the force could quickly pay their respects. It had been agreed with Barbara, so no toes were being trod upon.

As this day had turned out to be sunny and again very windy, Cutler and Williams thought it a nice idea to walk into town. Once again, passes had to be acquired, and a Colonel informed with what was going on. But there were no problems, and John Cutler was looking forward to the walk and then to meeting his friend's serving sons.

The walk was pleasant in the places that were sheltered, but when the wind hit them, they felt as if they could have taken off and flown down into the town. The pub was a nice old inn, and a fire greeted them as they entered. Williams was the first to spot the two likely seamen. Both had their uniforms on; they looked extremely smart and stood erect. They were over six foot, obviously kept very fit, probably by running or taking regular physical exercise; they sported a mop of blond hair, which made Cutler wonder if Steven had been blond in his younger days. Both came under the rank of Lieutenant Commanders, each being Captain of a Patrol Torpedo Boat.

Cutler went straight over, holding out his hand. "Am I looking at Steven's two small skinny tots, whom I haven't seen in all of twenty years?"

"Hello, nice to meet you; I am Andrew, this is Michael. We have been in touch with mum, so we have some idea of what has happened, but you can fill us in with the rest. What will you drink?" He looked at Williams first, then Cutler, and when the answer came back, Andrew caught the attention of the landlord and ordered.

"Two pints of your finest ale and two large Jamaican rums, please, landlord."

The four of them took four chairs and placed them close to the log fire that was giving off a pleasant warmth, along with that lovely sense of friendliness that open inglenook fireplaces can give. Cutler did not hold back: he liked Steven Harris, and now he liked his two sons. He told them everything: Cynthia Richmond, the two other girls, and all that led them here to Dover. He then told them that the killer was an integral part of a mission to Zeebrugge which should be leaving any day now, weather permitting. This last detail caused both the lads to look up sharply.

"You mustn't talk about the raid," said Michael in a rather alarmed voice.

"That is top secret; you could be in serious trouble for even mentioning that there is going to be a raid. Both our boats are involved in this skirmish too; we are there as rescue and support in general." He looked around to see if anyone had been listening, but then smiled to himself as there was no one else in the bar area. "What is the name of this man you think did the killings?"

"He is one Lieutenant David Bartlett, of the Royal Marines."

Michael looked at Andrew, rubbed his nose and raised his eyebrows in a gesture of slight bewilderment, but then followed on with, "I have never heard of him; there are several hundred Royal Marines involved. Are you really sure that this is the right man, that he is the fellow that is such an appalling murderer?"

"Not really any doubt about it, at least not in my or your father's mind. This is our man. But I cannot take him to trial unless he survives and comes back. So you can see why your father was so disturbed by all of this, and for your father's sake, and the rest of womanhood's, this man must hang for his terrible crimes."

They finished their drinks and all four had enjoyed one another's company, even with the knowledge that a fine man had died, and a serial criminal was about to get away with three terrible murders. They parted, the two sailors returning to the docks to oversee the work being completed on their crafts, Williams and Cutler to make that long hike back up to the barracks with nothing to do but wait.

XI

Finally the time had come for Lieutenant Bartlett to show his mettle. *HMS Vindictive*, that almost extinct battle cruiser which had been built in 1897, was starting to power up, still using coal to build up a head of steam for her engines; she was getting ready to proceed to the gathering point. Smoke was billowing out of her four funnels, and all and everything around her disappeared in the tarry acrid black fog that was being expelled; the effect that this had on people caught in it was very nasty: stinging the eyes, blackening the skin and making everyone cough badly. But of course, once in mid channel, moving in the currents of air that blew over the sea, things would not be so bad. She pulled slowly out into mid harbour; there a tug brought a huge tow rope, then another, which were quickly and safely tethered to the stern; these were going to be used to tow the two Mersey ferries, the *Royal Daffodil* and the *Royal Iris II*, whose value lay in their ability to carry several hundred men and land them close to shore, as these crafts had very shallow drafts. But it had been found that they were unstable in heavy seas, so it made sense to tow them. It might slow things down, but it was infinitely safer, and several hundred lives now depended on this towing to be successful.

HMS *Vindictive* would have been scrapped or used as a coaling vessel, which for a warship of the line, was without doubt an ignominious end to her existence, but now she was saved, and would be doing this one last journey, hopefully going down in the annals of naval history with great credit. She had been completely taken apart; everything that had any value, but was not essential to this last mission, was removed. All brass, copper, zinc and any other possible valuable metals were taken out; the feeling was that the Hun should not be allowed anything that could help his war effort. Only enough coal was stowed to complete the journey, and the worst and cheapest fuel was used. All the empty spaces were now taken up with solid concrete and rubble ballast, so that when she was scuttled, the Germans would have the devil's own job to empty her of this debris, with a view to either refloat her or break her up. Filling her up with the detritus had been the job given to Lieutenant Bartlett and his men, which they had performed with a will. At long last the job had been completed and the ship was now moving.

'Nothing will stop me now; I am on my way to destiny!'

Bartlett made sure that his men were comfortable, or at least as comfortable as they could get, considering there were no seats on which to sit, only hard iron flooring; there was precious little cover, as everything had been stripped away, but just like their officer, the men were happy to be now in action, or at this stage on their way to action. Bartlett visualised himself as Wellington just before the battle of Waterloo, or Nelson as he strode around the *Victory* at the battle of Trafalgar. This was *his* time, so he climbed to the topmost deck which retained the only major guns on this old tub, along with his own Lewis machine guns. His responsibility was to oversee the machine gunners in the forthcoming action. There he stood, facing into the wind; he knew how Caesar felt as the Romans crossed the English Channel to conquer a dark forbidding island called Britannia. And like his heroes he would be at the head of his army, thus making sure that his place in history was reserved, just for him.

The two Mersey ferries were now secured by huge ropes to the ageing cruiser and firmly held together too. These two ferries had been in loyal service for many years, taking hundreds of thousands of people backwards and forwards across from Birkenhead to Liverpool. When the Admiralty arrived in Liverpool to look at the two vessels with a view to using them specifically for this raid, they were delighted with what they found. Their condition was just right: they were double-hulled, so that they could bang into things without falling apart, and that made them pretty well unsinkable.

The draft that they used was extremely shallow: this was going to be perfect for the crossing of minefields.

Like on the *Vindictive* and the three block ships, everything that could be taken out was. Windows were boarded up; extra steel was placed strategically around so as to give more protection to the soldiers on board. But there would be no comfort whatsoever. These two ferries would carry plenty of coal, just so that they could make the journey back to Blighty after the raid had been successfully completed. Both were armed with machine guns and on their upper decks, they even sported flamethrowers, which were going to be used to keep any foolish German soldier from wanting to rush the ships in any nonsense counterattacks that they might think of doing. Never had two civilian ships been so heavily armed and encased in steel.

Gradually and very laboriously, the *Vindictive* made its way into mid-channel, careful and skilful enough to avoid the countless mines that were laid by the Allies to stop the Germans from doing to the Allies what the Allies were about to do to them. After two hours of manoeuvring, the small flotilla of boats and ships made up of four motor torpedo boats, submarines *C-1* and *C-3*, three aging cruisers: *HMS Thetis*, *HMS Iphigenia* and *HMS Intrepid*, along with some very fast launches to rescue anyone that might need their assistance, gathered for the journey up to the main rally point. This meeting area was at a location just off the Clacton-on-Sea shoreline. Anyone looking out that morning while walking their dog along the beach would have seen enough ships to make them think that they were witnessing Clacton's own 'Spithead Review'. Seventy-five ships and boats were now waiting for *HMS Vindictive* and its two charges to come to the head of three lines: it was going to be the honour of that old rusting cruiser to head the cast. That is if those ships astern did not all die of asphyxiation from the appalling choking smoke discharged from the four funnels, before they arrived off the Belgian coast. Poor old *Vindictive* was labouring terribly under the strain of having to pull two other vessels, and through using cheap tarry coal. At the very rear of the line of vessels sailed the new destroyer, *HMS Warwick*, the flagship which was to coordinate the entire operation. On board no less than Admiral Sir Roger Keyes was in charge.

When the signal came from Admiral Keyes, this motley band of ageing ships started out on their long laborious haul to Zeebrugge and Ostend. The time had actually come, the waiting was over: war was being brought to the U-boats instead of the other way round. Progress was slow, as the fastest they could travel was at the speed of the slowest ship. The launches and torpedo boats cruised around, always alert for signs of enemy shipping; they darted in and out of the line, like sheepdogs protecting their flock, using their superior speed to investigate any white-ridged wave in the distance, just in case it should turn out to be a submarine. The sea was choppy, not really rough, but heavy enough to make many of the marines and sailors on the smaller ships start feeling nauseous.

High on the open bridge stood Lieutenant Bartlett; he was dressed in his best officer's uniform; his shoes sparkled, so shiny one could see one's face in them, his trousers so neatly creased that one felt that one could use them as a knife, his dress jacket cleaned and pressed, buttons polished to a high sheen. He sported an officer's side arm, and knew that he would almost certainly be using it. Bartlett had made up his mind that the role which had been assigned to him as a Lewis gun operator and overseer was going to have to adapt to whatever situation evolved. He was determined to follow his path to glory, and not necessarily the assigned path.

He faced into the cold wind but was oblivious to any discomfort, enveloped as he was in the joy of now starting to fulfil his destiny. The Captain was also on that open bridge, but he was wrapped up in a heavy sheepskin overcoat, prepared for what the weather was going to throw at them; this applied to the marines and sailors too who also manned that part of the superstructure. Bartlett was a man with a mission: he did not care what the others thought of him, he was prepared for his death, and he intended to meet the scythe carrier with his head erect, wearing his best clothes.

At approximately a twenty mile distance from the shore the order was given to test fire the guns, and soon the entire fleet was shooting wildly into that green frothing brine. Bartlett called his two trusty Sergeants and gave the order for all his men to try out their rifles and Lewis guns, to lob the odd Mills bomb, and generally make a noise. Bartlett knew they would enjoy that. Everyone was very excited with the firing, and a great deal of laughter ensued; each white horse that was shot was in fact a Hun soldier. Not many Germans were actually disturbed by this testing of the armament, but a lot of fish swam away in a hurry.

After three hours had elapsed, the lines of ships had lengthened to approximately three miles, and the patrol boats where kept extremely busy, making sure that the slower ships tried to play catch up, because if any lucky U-boat Captain caught sight of this batch of slow moving craft, they would have a field day. There had been several supposed sightings of submarines, but as the torpedo boats investigated, none turned out to be the real thing, they were nothing but false alarms; yet each alert had to be taken seriously and checked, as if all their lives depended on it, which of course they did. Although it was April the wind still blew cold, coming from the north-east, which made it quite unusual for that time of year. The sea spray was now mixed with a drizzly rain, making it hard to decide which was worse. Still Bartlett faced into the wind, proud as a figurehead upon an old galleon. The other assembled members on the bridge had become aware of this strange officer, kitted out in his finest attire, more suited for a walk in the park with a pretty young lady on his arm on a sunny day than near-storm-condition seas. Yet, there he was, erect, dressed to the nines, upon a ship of war, ready to do battle. But nobody was going to say anything, each being lost in his own little world, wondering how he was going to perform and fretting whether he would let anyone or himself down. All, musing along those lines, except Lieutenant David Bartlett who knew precisely how he would fare.

The sky was now darkening; the sun which had stayed hidden all day was fast sinking below the horizon, and as it was cloudy and wet, it was going to be very dark indeed. Probably good for the attackers, making them hard to be seen by any enemy forces.

Another couple of hours went by, and Bartlett thought it was a good idea to see how his men were coping with the worsening conditions. Everything was dark upon the ship, and he had some difficulty locating them, but when he did, Sergeant Laker was giving a pep talk to calm any nerves that might be starting to fray at the edges. Bartlett need not have worried; his men looked fine, as far as he could tell, whereas he had long become dishevelled by the wind and rain.

"Are you warm enough, sir?" enquired Sergeant Laker. "You look as if you are freezing."

"Don't worry about me, I am fine; a little wind and rain never hurt anyone; anyway, to be perfectly honest, I like that feeling: it makes me feel alive. It has taken nearly four years in the service before having the chance to get at the Hun; I intend to enjoy every second of it, and that takes in going there and getting back to Dover afterwards. I know, Sergeant, that this is not going to be a cakewalk, but I am quite sure the Admiral knew what he was doing when he ordered the off. This is our chance to be heroes; we all have to take it when we can to achieve our goals in life, this is mine." He smiled in the direction of where he knew Laker was, but he could only make out the outline of the man. At that moment the ship shuddered severely as a huge wave lifted the bow out of the water and then threw it back down hard. Bartlett heard some of the men around heave as their stomachs reacted to the violent change in movement, but this was a problem for each individual person; there was nothing he could do.

"We must be close to the Belgian coast now; it should get much calmer once we are inshore. It should also be easier to see what is going on if the Germans start to hear our approach and send up star shells, or even turn on the land searchlights; so cheer up, chaps, you certainly will be able to see then, but it might be better for us if we didn't."

Bartlett made his way back up to the bridge; it was true, he thought he saw the occasional light from a house or fishing boat: that must be the Belgian coastline off to starboard; it was also true that the sea was getting calmer and the wind did seem to be dropping. Half an hour later, he knew he was right, as he could hear in the distance the guns of the two monitors that had been pounding various parts of the occupied coast over the last couple of weeks, strutting their stuff yet again. The damage caused was probably negligible; most of the shells in all likelihood landed harmlessly in the sand dunes that abounded in that part of the coast, but damage wasn't really their purpose. The idea was to get the enemy used to their shelling, so that tonight would be no different from any other evening, thus giving the attackers the edge that they so desperately needed: surprise... Their huge sixty pounder shells kept crashing into the coastal areas, and like most other nights, the German defenders were laughing at the pointlessness of the bombardment.

Eleven o'clock came, and *HMS Vindictive* slowed her engines which almost sighed with relief. The two ferries *Daffodil* and *Iris* were finally freed of the bonds, and now under their own steam, they started, albeit temporarily, to make their way ahead of *Vindictive*, giving the rest of the fleet time to close ranks. The few ships that were going to Ostend had long departed, and before the attack would be waiting for the witching hour, just as the Zeebrugge ships were now doing. The launches, torpedo boats and the rest of the patrol craft were now waiting just a few miles off the harbour, before they could start the planned release of the smoke that the firework king, 'Brock', had devised. He had produced a chemical made from saccharin, the very same substance used as a sweetener by obese and diabetic people. The government had managed to acquire the entire stock that was stored in Britain, so a lot of people from now on, were going to be drinking their tea and coffee unsweetened. But the substance that he had devised, once injected into exhaust chambers, created the most incredible black, and very toxic, smoke. This was to drift into the harbour areas of Zeebrugge and Ostend, making it impossible for the defenders to see the oncoming ships.

The two monitors were busy doing their work; shells were heading landward at a speed that surprised all ships as they passed by those two flat floating platforms with their heavy guns. How proud Keyes felt knowing that the men operating those huge cannons were working their particular fingers to the bone and breaking all records in their rate of fire.

The three block ships were brought up to the front of the line; *Thetis* and *Intrepid* had fared badly on the journey over: with only a skeleton crew manning the vessel, things had got very sticky once or twice when water had flooded into various parts of the two ships, unseen; in fact *Thetis* was now showing a list of around twenty-five degrees to the port side, and the remaining working pumps were busy syphoning water to keep the ship afloat. But the goal was close now; nobody seriously thought that either of the cement-filled block ships would not make their objective. All three were going to give the U-boats and their Captains a serious headache, or bust trying.

Bartlett looked at his wristwatch: ten to twelve; the old cruisers that were going to block the entrances to the main canal route to Brugge were now positioned, bows firmly facing towards the harbour area of Zeebrugge. Though they were still three miles out, they could quite clearly see the outline of the world's longest man-made fixed object, the mole.

It was at this point that the two monitors changed direction of fire, laying a broader fan of shells, this time specifically towards Zeebrugge harbour area.

The mole structure was stretching out for one and a half mile from the south side of the canal area into the North Sea in a banana shape. It was made from solid granite, so was expected to be there for a little time yet! A thousand foot long wooden viaduct structure that was there to let tidal surges through linked the mole to the beach. At the end of the mole a lighthouse which had been switched off since 1914 was standing prominently right at the end of a hundred foot pier. *HMS Vindictive* had to berth just landward side of that pier, disgorge the Marines whose job it was to knock out all the defences, then hold the mole until the entire task of blocking the canal entrance was completed, and finally ram itself between the block ships if space needed filling. Other Marines would be landed at various stages along the mole, either by the two ferries or by some other craft that had been brought along for this purpose. Everything was now ready; all they had to wait for was twelve o'clock, the witching hour, then the two attacks would start simultaneously, at Ostend and at Zeebrugge. The Captain piped every soldier to action stations; guns were checked, and then checked again. As there was no seating since all chairs and furniture had been removed weeks before, all Marines were told to sit on the floor or deck wherever they happened to be, in anticipation of the incoming fire and possible injuries.

Sergeant Laker drew all his men around him, then having quietened them said:

"Now remember, men, keep close to the concrete parapet on the mole, make directly for each manned bunker, and eliminate the enemy as quickly as you can, then move onto the next and so on. But at all times keep your heads down; and be reminded that bullets kill, don't catch any!" He smiled to himself in the darkness of the ship, and then remembered a joke that he had heard in the Sergeants' mess on a previous day; he thought it might be a good idea to keep the men relaxed with a little story.

"I want to tell you all a little story, while we are waiting for the start of the attack. Three old ladies lived together in an old rickety house; all were going slightly doolally. The oldest, called Agatha, went up the stairs to the bathroom, drew out enough hot water to fill the bath, got undressed and looked at the water... 'Did I draw that water to have a bath? Have I had a bath, do I need a bath? I had better ask Gertrude'. She called down the stairs and asked Gertrude if she would come up, and tell her if she had already been in the bath or whether she should be going in it?' Gertrude walked up the stairs, got half way up and stopped; she looked up, then down, and thought to herself, 'I remember that Agatha called me up the stairs to see if she had washed or needed to wash, whether she had been in the bath, or needed to go into the bath, but did I do it, did I tell her or do I still have to tell her; in fact, am I going up the stairs or coming down?' She called down to Gwen. 'Gwen, am I half way up the stairs, or am I half way down? Agatha called me up to see if she needed a bath or whether she had already had one? But for the life of me, I cannot remember if I have been up to tell her and coming down, or whether I still have to go up to see if she should be in that blasted bath; can you help?' Gwen went red with anger, and then shouted back to Gertrude and Agatha, 'What a pair of idiots you both are; why you both are so stupid, I believe you are as thick as this...' She then brought her fist firmly down onto the wooden table, immediately looked up and said... 'Was that someone at the back door or the front?'"

There was a great deal of laughter from the men, followed by more jokes and more laughter. The tension had been broken. Laker knew he had to thank Bartlett for the psychology that he and Sergeant Riley used on the men to keep the morale high, and it worked.

Lieutenant Bartlett looked once more at his watch: twelve o'clock; this was the time of the attack. He knew that there were now fifteen hundred men at this precise moment all gearing themselves up for the melee that was now approaching fast.

The signal was sent out and the torpedo and patrol launches started injecting their exhausts with 'Brock's' concoction. Smoke billowed out as requested and started to drift to the harbour area and shore. All of a sudden, the silence around them was broken: guns burst into life, flashes could be seen from the tracer shells, all heading towards enemy targets, or so the gunners hoped. At first it was just one way, but soon shells from the shore batteries started seeking out the flotilla. It was now time for the two ferries and *Vindictive* to make their way towards the mole.

Things at first went well: all the attacking craft were closing onto the mole and harbour without being seen. They could discern through the choking smoke that the Germans were sending up rockets to try and see where the attackers were, but at that moment the Hun was in the fog. Just when the ships were less than a few hundred yards from their objective the smoke cleared as the wind changed, pushing the black clouds back onto the launches. Now the attackers could be seen; once again rocket flares were sent skywards, this time lighting all the vessels with a ghostly pallor, and then it started in all seriousness. The Hun obviously knew they were coming, as almost every yard of the mole was taken up with storm-troopers firing machine guns; the bigger guns that were ensconced upon the granite structure now found a good reason to open up on targets that could be clearly seen. A large shell immediately hit the *Vindictive*, killing most of the crew manning Lewis guns at the stern of the ship. Then another, and another, whooshed over the sea, hitting all parts of the vessel. The Captain who was a very brave man was one of the first to be wounded, but he would not leave his post and managed to steer the cruiser onwards towards the mole. There were explosions going on everywhere around him; he steered in the direction of the spot he thought they should be landing at, but he was off course by at least five hundred yards. *HMS Vindictive* hit the quayside with a slight crash, but it was enough to unbalance all that were still standing. Moreover, the ship had created a huge wave, which after hitting the quay returned, slamming into the old cruiser, pushing it back out; this went on for several minutes, while all the time shells were bursting through the ship, and over it in the form of shrapnel, along with many high explosives which where doing their deadly duty.

Machine gun fire was also spluttering all over the craft. Many men were killed or wounded from the onset, but nobody seemed to have any idea on how they could get the *Vindictive* to settle against the mole. Men were running frantically about, all trying to land some rope lines onto the mole, but without success. The incoming light fire from the German storm troopers was having a very demoralising effect on the attackers, and many were now cowering behind some metal structure or anything that would give them some form of shelter from the bullets. Bartlett saw his moment come: this was the start of *his* time. He went straight to a fallen rifle near by dropped by a luckless Marine that had been hit in the first wave of bullets; he saw a target: a very foolish German sitting on the top of the mole, firing at anything and everything; he made the perfect target. *Crack*, went his gun; the Hun fell backwards losing his helmet as he fell. A Marine attached to Bartlett's unit watched and cheered as if this had been the first enemy soldier to catch one in return.

The confusion was pervading, not just on the *Vindictive*; soldiers and sailors from all the ships were coming under intense fire, and the death and injury rate was already higher than expected. But the flotilla was laying a fine barrage and doing unto the Hun what the Hun was doing to them. Shoreline batteries were the heaviest, and their shells were inflicting the biggest damage when they hit a vessel: it was not just armour piercing shells, but high explosive that once through the steel hull, would then explode, killing and maiming crew and Marines alike.

Bartlett had not been idle during the confusion. He had got his Lewis gun firing and knew he had hit something when the firing from that point abruptly stopped. The problem was that somehow the tides had not been taken into consideration, and the bridge was too low for most of its guns to fire successfully onto the mole. *Vindictive* was taking a terrible pounding and was barely able to retaliate with a mild slap in return. Some of the heavy shelling came from large guns on the shoreline, dug well in the sand dunes. Several big rounds hit amidships, puncturing the engine room, causing yet more serious casualties and deaths. Fortunately, none of these shells fell beneath the waterline and did no serious damage to the engines themselves.

Bartlett now frustrated with not being able to aim at anything, turned and saw that many of the men on the bridge were in a terrible state. Without giving a thought to bullets and shells, he busied himself with moving the badly wounded to a safer position, and making sure that the dead were in fact just that. The Captain was still struggling with the wheel, trying hard to keep the ship from yet again causing a wave that would only push her out anew. Then help came in the guise of *HMS Daffodil*: that plucky little ferry was now being positioned by its Captain to push the *Vindictive* into the mole's granite walling, and then hold it there. At last the ship was up against their objective and it was time for it to disgorge all its Marines. That became the next problem: the landing gangways, all ten of them, which had been specially erected on the sides of the *Vindictive*, had been damaged by the defending shelling; only two were anywhere near operational, and having to deal with only these two, made the defenders's job much easier. But one way or another, the attackers must land and take the positions.

Bartlett saw his moment; he jumped down from the bridge directly onto the mole, which straight away attracted fire. Bullets whizzed all around him, but somehow he managed to take a rope that could pull one of the gangways down from the position in which it was hung. It crashed heavily onto the mole and several men rushed up, firing as they went. The first man was one of Bartlett's own men; he recognised him as Private Tring, but as the man rushed past Bartlett who was still holding the rope, Tring attracted fire and was hit. He then fell over clutching his stomach; Bartlett saw that he was still alive, as he was thrashing around in agony. Without a second thought, while other Marines were now spilling onto the mole and firing back at the Hun, he went to the aid of Private Tring. Picking him up bodily, he lifted him over the side, and down to willing hands to get him below decks and out of the way of more injuries.

At that precise moment Bartlett felt a hot sensation pass through his thigh, then a sharp pain: he had been hit by rifle fire. He jumped, but as he could still walk, he managed to make his way to the parapet of the mole, and on the way picked up Tring's rifle. He followed the few men that had successfully made it onto the mole, and watched, as they took the first of many machine gun nests. Then he saw that another man had fallen; using his rifle as a crutch, he dragged the luckless soldier by the scruff of his collar back towards the *Vindictive*, where once again he lowered him over the side to more willing hands. All the time, firing was coming from almost every German in the Kaiser's entire army. Several of the big guns on the *Vindictive* opened up on the beach targets, these being the open dugouts where large calibre cannons could actually be seen. One of the German beach guns was quite obviously hit when a huge explosion briefly lit the whole area: the shell must have struck an ammunition dump for the gun. A fire resulted, which clearly showed the gunners more German targets to fire at, which they did with enthusiasm. At last the attacking Allies were finding that it was possible to get their teeth stuck into the rear end of a Hun soldier, and they enjoyed that feeling.

Bartlett tried to move yet again towards his men; he picked up the rifle, this time so that he could fire it, but he could not: his trigger finger on his right hand was no longer there. He stopped, looked at his hand in wonderment, and then started to laugh out loud. 'If this is all you feel when you get killed, bring it on!' He dropped the now useless gun, pulling out of his ammunition belt a couple of Mills bombs instead. Blood was pouring from the two wounds, but he was not at all worried by the loss of the red stuff of life; after all, this was his destiny, and he was enjoying it all as if he was at a fun fair. With his left hand he drew the pin of a grenade and threw the Mills bomb in the direction of where he thought some enemy guns were firing from. But the subsequent explosion startled even him; yet why it should, he did not understand. What with machine gun fire and shell fire, what was a grenade explosion doing being heard? He then realised that he had become completely detached from all the surrounding noise, apart from what he was doing, or about to do. He did not even feel the need to run, not that he was now able to, but he could still hobble; after all, it did not matter how many times he got hit, he would still be able to carry on; nothing, not even bullets, were going to stop him.

Daffodil was still pushing the aged cruiser *Vindictive* into the mole, but that meant that the Marines aboard her were now stuck there. It was too much for them to climb from the ferry onto the cruiser, then onto the mole. Shells were also bursting onto that Mersey wonder; one had crashed through the double hull, and burst in the engine room, killing one stoker. Machine gun fire was strafing her exposed decks, and those that were

148

caught on that outside area were soon meeting their maker. Dead and wounded were lying everywhere; it was fast becoming a turkey shoot for the Germans.

HMS *Iris*, the other Mersey ferry, had fared better, and landed at the right spot on the mole. Most of the one hundred and fifty Marines had managed to land, and had scampered along, neutralising the entire machine gun nests that proliferated at the end of the mole and across the pier up to the lighthouse. The Germans had even set up trench mortars; unfortunately for them, most of the bombs they had fired from their mortars had fallen harmlessly into the sea, once again killing innocent marine life. But one mortar did fall amongst some onrushing Marines, killing at least eight and wounding many more. Yet the defenders were being eliminated, even if it was only one by one. Many wounded Marines were now able to be rescued and taken back aboard the *Iris*: they had done their duty. So the Marines now held the lighthouse area and the pier, but they were still attracting incoming fire as far away as the shore, and the shells that were being lobbed into their midst were huge sixty pounders: when they exploded, they did not take prisoners. As a shell came in and hit the mole itself, the huge chunks of concrete that were being displaced caused massive injuries when pieces hit the attacking soldiers. The wounds became very serious indeed.

While the fighting was taking place at the mole, the *Thetis*, *Iphigenia* and *Intrepid* were slowly making their way to the canal entrance. But their good fortune was, like for all the other combatants, about to change for the worse. The Germans had waited until they were reasonably close, and then opened with everything that was available. The three ships were hit with heavy shells all over their superstructure. The bridge on the *Iphigenia* was almost completely blown away, making steering the crippled block ship an impossible task.

All three of these old obsolete cruisers were manned by the minimum crew needed, and each man had volunteered to be there. Though the shells were smashing into each of the three vessels, the casualties were slighter than for the other ships, purely because there were fewer sailors to hit. Yet the damage was great, and all three had been hit many times below the water line. It was going to take a minor miracle for them to reach their destination. But each Captain was extremely determined; after all, they hadn't come all this way, lost so many sailors to just end up sunk in an open part of the harbour area; it had to be the canal or they would all die trying.

At the same time as all this commotion was going on at various parts of the Zeebrugge harbour, the two submarines were trying to get to their position under the viaduct. Both were packed with ammonal, a very highly charged robust explosive that took little to set it off. Their job was to jam themselves under the viaduct, then set the charges to blow the submarines while the skeleton crew made good its escape. Both of the underwater craft came down the seaward side of the mole as cautiously as possible. The Hun knew they were coming as they had been spotted, but they waited until they were close enough to blow them both out of the water. This was one part of the plan that the defenders did not know about, so when they did start firing, and both craft were hit on many occasions, they were close enough to the viaduct to crash straight in and under it.

C-1 was the first to set the charge and the crew managed to get out and onto a rubber raft that had been fastened to the side of the boat. Unfortunately the charge did not go off, so *C-3* had to try the same tactic. She crashed headlong into and under the viaduct almost beside *C-1*; the Commander set the charge, and quickly ordered his men to abandon ship. They had gone no more than fifty yards from the vessel when it blew, which also made *C-1* blow up as well. For once the plan had worked: the viaduct was a smashed, twisted mass of metal; no counterattacking soldiers were going to cross over that in a hurry. The life raft carrying the crew of *C-3* had been close by when she blew; luck being their middle name, debris rained everywhere, happily missing both rafts. But the defenders were not thrilled about this and opened up with machine gun fire on both the inflatable life rafts. Everyone sustained a wound, but once again luck was a fine mistress to be wooing, and no one died from their injuries. Soon, they were quite a long way out, badly hurt, but alive. A coastal motor launch called *HMS Polygon*, commanded by one Lieutenant Commander Michael Harris saw the two rafts, quickly assessed that their situation was dangerous to say the least, so came aside and rescued the men on board. Michael, mourning the death of his father, came alive again, knowing he had saved eight souls from certain death.

Lieutenant David Bartlett was starting to feel pain from the hole in his thigh. Blood had oozed consistently, and now a feeling of nausea was making its presence felt. The pain was not unbearable, it was more a dull ache, but the onset of weakness from the loss of blood was worrying him considerably.

'I am not finished yet; there are things I must still do', then the thought 'atone' came into his mind. For the first time, he started to think of the pretty young women whom he had slaughtered in a quite matter-of-fact way, as if it was his special right to do so; only now did he ponder, and this brooding came as a shock to him. At first he dismissed the thoughts, then as these horrors kept reappearing in his mind, he had a revelation. 'Of course, I am dying; this is why I must make amends, I must make atonement for the girls I killed. One way I can do that is to be as brave as I can while I am here on this earth. My men need me, and I will not let them down. I don't mind leaving this world; I am prepared to meet my maker, but I must complete what I was put down here for. I shall die a hero at Zeebrugge.'

With a struggle he got to his feet once more, then immediately was knocked down again. A bullet had passed cleanly through his left shoulder taking flesh and bone, coming out the other side. Again he felt no pain, but that did not surprise him anymore; he was being handed the chance of redemption, and he would *not* let any higher power down. He struggled to his feet; shells and bullets were zinging around him, tracer could be seen everywhere. There were so many pieces of lead in the air at one time, one could not fail to expect every living thing to fall dead or wounded at that very moment. But the Hun was taking fire too, not to the same extent, but big shells were coming in from the destroyer out at sea that Admiral Keyes was using as his command post; besides which, all the rest of the fleet were pounding various parts of the harbour and shoreline. Bartlett moved in a crab-like fashion along the mole towards the viaduct area: there were still machine gun nests to put out of action. He came across a dead Marine, not one of his own, but a Marine nevertheless. The poor fellow had a flamethrower pack on his back. Usually this would be better suited for two able men to use properly, but when needs must...

Bartlett turned the lad over so as to remove the pack, and then with a tremendous feat of will, he managed to get it onto his own back. Now dragging himself and the heavy gear, he strained towards a position where a machine gun nest had been. He was still being fired at from the shore, but he would not be visible in this nest. The Lieutenant dragged the remains of two Hun soldiers out of the way so that he could have a clear shot at the next nest. The pain from his wounds was exacerbated by the huge effort he was demanding from his body. He leaned over the top of the parapet, took careful aim, and then unleashed the devil's fire. For a second he heard nothing except the sound of escaping flame, then above that, came an appalling scream which curdled what blood he had left in his veins. He moved on towards the next nest. Some other Marine had come up behind him, and one soldier whom he knew as Thomas Barnes, a footballer in peace time who had played for Aldershot Football Club, asked him:

"Sir, you have been hit, let me take the flame thrower; you need to get back for treatment."

"Don't worry about me, we all have our duty to do, so let's get on with it! But you can take this awful contraption; it is hurting my left shoulder something chronic."

"I am not surprised, sir, you have a wound there, and you are bleeding quite a lot; in fact you have several wounds." Barnes looked at the Lieutenant in wonderment. "You seem to be bleeding from three places. Sir, let me get you back to the ship." But at that moment, a German mortar burst not more than twenty feet away, and Barnes along with two other Marines fell to the mole in agony, as shrapnel had entered their bodies. Lieutenant Bartlett had been shielded from the worst of the blast by Barnes, who now lay at his feet slithering in great pain, moaning and staring wildly. Bartlett knew he could not pick him up, but at least he could drag him. He looked around to see where the nearest point of safety was; it turned out to be a small launch that had come towards the mole with the purpose of removing wounded and dying soldiers. The Lieutenant once again took Barnes, like the others, by the scruff of the neck and started to drag himself and his fellow Marine towards where the coastal motor boat was coming about. It took a whole five minutes to get to the edge; bullets were continuously ricocheting around them both, but this time neither was hit.

"Come closer and I will lower him down to you, much closer, I only have one good arm."

The craft came right up to where Bartlett was leaning over. He pulled Barnes up to the edge, then taking a deep breath the Lieutenant grabbed the ex-footballer once again. He took a really hard bite with his good arm at the collar, and then pushed the man over the side to swing, while still holding him tight. Willing hands plucked Barnes and took him aboard.

"Lieutenant, now you!" a voice called to him from the launch.

"No, not yet! There are two more Marines badly wounded, hang on where you are while I get them."

"Well, be quick about it, we are attracting fire onto ourselves here," came the worried voice.

He knew he was just about done in, and that last effort had made him bleed badly from all his wounds. 'Three men saved! Will that make reparation for the last three women I killed?' He knew tears were welling up inside him, and for the first time, he had a perception that maybe what he had done had been wrong? He was aware that whatever he did now might make him feel better, but it would not bring any of the girls back to life.

Again, he mustered some more strength, and started to crawl back to where the other two were both laying and bleeding. He made it to the nearest, did not recognise him, did not wait to be introduced, but grabbed his collar too. This time it took at least six minutes to reach the side and call to the boat again. Marshalling hidden reserves he yet again managed to lower the man over the side to safety. Now streams of tears were flowing down his cheeks, and he was crying openly.

"Save yourself, man, you will not be able to manage the last!"

Lieutenant David Bartlett did not even hear him, but turned away crawling towards the last Marine. How he managed to pull him to the edge, nobody knew; to onlookers it was a miracle, to Bartlett it was just making sure that his destiny was being fulfilled. Once more, with superhuman effort, he dragged the now unconscious Marine to the edge, tried to lower him, but the boat moved away when a wave pushed it out. Bartlett was left screaming for the Commander to get that bloody craft in and take the wounded man from him. This was done, and again a voice called out.

"For pity's sake, throw yourself over, we will rescue you. Come on, you have done your duty, you are a bloody hero. Get down here!"

There were huge explosions detonating all around; bullets, shells, mortars, and grenades were flying everywhere: the entire mole was one great big shambles. Men were screaming from the pain of being hit whilst the granite was running red with British blood. Bartlett did not hear any of these noises; he knew he was dying, and he wanted to do just that. His destiny had been fulfilled; what else was there to live for? Anyway, if he made it back to Blighty, what would be waiting for him... the gallows?

He did hear one last thing as he tried to raise himself from that leaning position over the edge of the mole; it was a loud *crack*, and yet another bullet entered his body, this time almost centre of his stomach. This was it, and he knew he was slipping quickly into oblivion. He looked up at the sky for one last time; a German star shell burst overhead, lighting up the whole harbour once again.

'Damn, I would like to have seen the stars one last time'. He then fell forward and died.

The three rusting cruisers, with their ballast of concrete and rubble, were still trying hard to make it into the canal entrance. Each ship had been hit dozens of times, and all three were very close to sinking. If they didn't make that canal, then the entire operation would have been for nothing. The entrance was now less than one hundred yards away. *HMS Thetis* had been hit too many times below the water line to make the canal, and when the Captain heard that the engine room was now awash, and that the remaining boiler could quite easily blow up, he ordered the sailors up topside, ready to abandon ship. Shells were still smashing every part of the super-structure, and many of the skeleton crew had already been killed or very seriously wounded. The problem solved itself as the stern gently settled, dragging on the harbour bottom. She was finished, now completely stopped in her tracks; with yet more shells pounding into her, she quickly followed the stern and rested quietly but firmly on the soft mud below her. Sadly, she had not managed to reach a position that would affect the coming or going of any U-boats. For the *Thetis* this entire journey had been nothing but a waste of human life.

Just about every available working shore gun was firing at the two remaining block ships. *HMS Iphigenia* was now very close to the entrance, but she too was starting to settle in the water; she needed to survive just another minute of the pounding from the shells, and if by then she hadn't slipped below the waves, she would be at the target position. *HMS Intrepid* was somehow protected from most of the explosions, as she was sheltered somewhat, being just behind *Iphigenia*. A new tack from the shore batteries began with the concentration of shelling on the superstructure, hoping to knock out the steering of the cruiser. Fortunately it was too late: she had entered the canal entrance and her speed had increased to five knots, so that whatever hit her now, her weight and speed were going to get her to the designated spot for the blocking. But with that increased speed she was now making waves which washed from one side of the canal to the other, and then came back, rocking the ship, making it almost impossible to control. The Captain tried to bring her sideways on, but only managed to take the bow into a mud bank, and instead of the stern coming round, it too just ran aground. It had partially blocked the canal, but any U-boat Captain worth his salt would realise he only had to wait for high tide and then he could manoeuvre his craft around the hulk, encountering few problems. It was all or nothing for *Intrepid*. She too had gained extra speed, and the idea was to bring her up close to the *Iphigenia*, but her steering had been blown away a second or two before. Once again, the Gods had been cruel to the Allies. She was now out of control, but instead of crashing into the *Iphigenia* she drifted to her port side and hit another mud bank; there her stern did come around a little, nearly blocking the channel. Again, unfortunately, it was pretty well all for nothing: high tides would solve all the U-boats problems.

On being informed of the dubious outcome of the fleet's night work, Admiral Keyes called for a general retreat. Everyone that could be saved would be. Both the *Daffodil* and the *Iris* came off lightly with very little structural damage, and this was partly due to the way they were both made, with double hulls; they were built to withstand potential crashing into quays and docks. Many of the Marines that were aboard both these vessels survived with minor injuries. Once the *Daffodil* pulled back from *HMS Vindictive*, she too, quickly reversed to make her escape. The whole of the cruiser's superstructure was seriously damaged, and many of her men had been caught by the first rage of the battle. Though she was still seaworthy, she was in a mess. Dead, dying and injured lay everywhere. It was going to take a miracle to get this floating rust bucket back to Dover, but she must get back, and fast, or there were going to be more dead bodies than live ones on board; the Captain had been indeed forced to make a quick reassessment of their particular situation. The original plan had been to use the *Vindictive* as the final part in the jigsaw, her role being to end up as the meat between the sandwich by sinking her in the canal entrance alongside the other three blockships. But, because of the tremendous loss of life and additionally, the inability of the

Daffodil to land her Marines, the old cruiser was carrying too many dead and wounded to contemplate leaving them to sink along with the vessel. She was now going to have to struggle back to Dover with her human cargo. This was going to be tough going, as she had only been coaled with enough fuel for a one way trip. If necessary, she too, could be towed. Following the two ferries, she quickly pulled back and into the open sea; her fight tonight was well and truly over, but yet she persisted in firing from what guns still worked, using up her remaining ammunition.

The torpedo boats and the coastal motor launches were being kept frantically busy, some making their way to the mole to take off survivors, while other harassed the foe with everything they could throw at them. It had not gone all of Germany's way; they too had lost many men, and many guns, big and small. But the objectives had not been met; the channels were still open to enemy shipping. As quickly as they came, the fast inshore boats left, carrying off their cargo of survivors; there was nothing for the Marines left stranded behind to do but surrender, and this they did. The block ships crew members that could not be rescued managed to clamber ashore, to be taken into captivity.

HMS Polygon had been the launch designated to be at the mole side to rescue the wounded Marines that Bartlett had managed to hand down. Lieutenant Commander Michael Harris had watched all the goings-on at the mole and had felt sickened by the disaster that seemed to be unfolding; that was until he saw the heroics that one Marine Lieutenant was performing, trying so hard to save his men, all the while being under fire and wounded. 'The man is a bally hero! He must be saved at all costs; I have never seen or heard of such bravery before!' Tears of sadness, and yet at the same time joy, welled within him. He had been privileged enough to witness true British 'Boy's Own' heroism at its most British best. He was proud to be there and be a part of this terrible, but incredibly foolish melee that in his opinion would go down as one of the great British battles of the time.

Nonsense, but wonderfully British nonsense!

He had witnessed this officer sacrifice himself, quite selflessly, to save his men, whom he must have had the greatest respect for, and one hoped vice versa. He saw three men being saved from certain death, and then the Lieutenant had been shot once again, right in front of him. Bartlett had been on the edge of the mole so that when he fell lifeless, he fell off into the sea.

'At the very least I can save his body from the Hun or the fish; let's bring him on board.'

He ordered one of his seamen to lean over the side and bring the body onto the launch, so that it could have a fine military burial on shore in England, where he belonged. The sailor duly did as he was bid, and dragged the lifeless body of Lieutenant David Bartlett on board. He was laid on the deck, for all to see; a hero is a very rare commodity, and one cannot get too much of such people. *Polygon* sped out to sea, quickly catching up with the departing remaining fleet. Though all the sailors were on continuous watch for U-boats or other enemy ships, Harris decided to see who the brave Marine was. He walked over to the body, and then leaned over to look at the face. He jumped back in amazement, as there had been definite movement from the corpse.

"Jones, you are a medic. This man is a bloody superman, he is not dead. Get over here and plug him up; and bloody well keep him alive!"

Dawn was breaking over the horizon when East Anglia was sighted by the Destroyer *HMS Warwick*. It was a reddish yellow dawn, but calm and serene; even the sea tried hard not to hinder the fleet as it made its way back across the North Sea to the safer waters of the British Channel. Admiral Keyes was elated, not knowing the full outcome of the raid; failure was not a word in his vocabulary, and like many a war leader before him, his mind had managed to turn disaster into victory. He had witnessed the three rusting cruisers enter the harbour area and heard reports that at least two had made it to the canal; in his mind this meant those two would have blocked that accursed waterway from the enemy submarines. For Keyes their night had been a satisfying success: it was just like the charge of the '*Light Brigade*' at Balaclava, in which the British charged into a valley where the Russian cannons were known to be positioned on three sides; yet they still managed to break the enemy and capture a major gun position. This event took place during the Crimean War, and in its own way the raid on Zeebrugge and Ostend would also go down in history as a glorious sacrifice.

The depleted fleet kept close to the shipping lanes that were mine free, but stayed always alert for any enemy submarines that might be lurking, just on the off chance that ships would be using them. Keyes whistled down to the wardroom on the *Warwick*, demanding that scrambled eggs, bacon and sausages be immediately placed on the menu for breakfast: he would be down to sample within a few minutes. The chefs were to make sure that everybody on board got the same treatment: a star breakfast for one and all. He rubbed his tummy, smacked his lips, smiled at the Captain on the bridge and said, "Captain, will you join me, please?"

The two ferries, *Iris* and *Daffodil*, were struggling hard to keep pace with the rest of the returning ships. Even though it was comparatively calm, for North Sea weather, it was still throwing these two vessels around like corks in a storm. It had been better when they had been towed, as they had not been built for crossing major seas, but merely major rivers. Ferries didn't sport proper galleys, so whatever food was going to be eaten as breakfast was going to be hard to prepare. A hundred loaves of bread, a small mountain of butter, and boxes upon boxes of '*Ticklers*' plum and apple jam had been brought along. They could make strong sweet tea, mainly using steam from one of the boilers, but it almost gave a rather rusty tang to the taste. Each boat carried a doctor, and several medical nurses, all men; these were there to handle any wounded that were brought back on board; and in the case of *Iris*, there were many; on *Daffodil* there were five, of which four had been pulled out of the sea. All five were in a state of shock. The breakfast was a great success; everyone needed that buzz that the sugar gave them, especially from the 'Ticklers' jam.

This scene was being played out on every ship, including all the small craft, though on the torpedo boats and the coastal motor boats which carried less people, it was harder to cater for those on board as they crashed over waves at high speed.

Admiral Keyes heard of the brave feats that his sailors and Marines had accomplished, and along with his number two, was working out how many men were due to obtain medals for what had taken place. He even suggested that several should be awarded VCs. All the while that Keyes was dealing with rewards for a supposed job well done the Germans were now working their way across the three hulks to see what was going to be the quickest way to remove them completely from the canal channel and the harbour area. On the very first high tide after the raid, three U-boats left the safety of Brugge canal, working their way down to the lock gates which remained completely undamaged, and then passing the *Iphigenia* and the *Intrepid*, slid out silently into the North Sea to carry the war to the Allies. Nothing had changed, there was merely minor damage that could and would easily be repaired, along with a lot of dead and wounded combatants. And while the mangled areas were already being made good, four hundred men were being taken into captivity in Germany: their war was over.

HMS Vindictive was leaking water into her keel, but the pumps were managing to keep her afloat. The cruiser had been hit several hundred times, and though the superstructure was a tangled mess of metal and wood, she could still keep pace with the rest of the fleet. Sadly, *Vindictive* carried the most bodies; as it had been the first into the fray, she caught the worst of what was thrown at them; how the vessel stayed afloat was a minor miracle, thanks to the determination of a fine crew. But she was making it, for there, not more than five miles away, was the port of Dover; then she could berth and disgorge her human cargo. All her guns were more or less out of action now, either through damage by incoming shell fire, or worn-out barrels after the hundreds of rounds sent back to the foe. Amazingly, after all the hours that had elapsed since leaving Zeebrugge and the stopping of firing, the inside of the barrels was still warm enough to take the chill out of any cold hand that was placed inside. Those men that were not on duty watching out for enemy were sound asleep anywhere they could lay their heads. Even the cold morning wind couldn't wake that contingent of sleeping warriors.

At last, Dover came into view, much to the relief of many of the ships' Commanders, and HMS *Vindictive* was the first to find a berth, then start unloading her wounded and dead. Many of the Marines who had been under the command of Lieutenant Bartlett had been killed or injured, and at least fifteen had been left on the mole, either dead or captured by the Germans. It would be several months before news filtered through as to their fate. The Captain, who had also been slightly hit in the shoulder by shrapnel, started to look over the vessel he had commanded; he wondered how firstly she had taken so much fire without actually sinking, then how they actually managed to steer her to their home port. He walked around with his mouth agape, staring at this smashed part of the structure or that, shaking his head in disbelief at the damage. Whilst still in the middle of it, he had not had time to assess just how bad things had got. On leaving the ship he wandered over to where the wounded were waiting for ambulances to come and take them directly to hospitals in the area. Occasionally he recognised someone, and if they were conscious, he went up, shook their hand, thanked them for their contribution and wished them well and a quick return to action. He was a good man, and liked by all his subordinates; he treated men well, and got respect in return. As he walked along that line of men, he came across a Sergeant that he had seen taking the fight to the Hun; he went to him with a smile on his face.

"Sergeant, allow me to shake your hand. I saw you take out a machine gun nest all on your own, and I was very impressed, then I saw you shoot several Germans who were trying hard to reach that very same nest, and you were unlucky enough to stop a bullet. I am going to recommend that you get some recognition for your brave acts. Tell me, what is your name?"

"Sergeant Laker, sir, and thank you for your kind words."

"You must also tell me who that officer was that dragged you back to the *Vindictive. Crikey*, his performance was nothing short of a miracle and he seemed to be getting away with it. It wasn't just you that were saved, but at least two or three more. Then that officer seemed to have got himself shot or took shrapnel; in all the firing and mayhem, he just disappeared. I rather guess that his fate was decided by death or capture, which is a crying shame: his exploits indeed merited recognition."

"That was our officer, Lieutenant David Bartlett. Like me, sir, that was his first taste of action, but believe me when I tell you that his men love him, and would have followed him into the jaws of hell, if asked."

"A fine fellow, a fine fellow. Well, Bartlett, eh? I shall remember that name too, and make sure that something comes to him, even if it is posthumously; he really deserved a medal."

Laker lay back on the stretcher and thought how Bartlett had led by example, sighed, hoped he was still alive, but rather doubted it; he then sank into a dream, mentally and physically exhausted.

By the time most of the dock was cleared of the wounded, the final boat came through the harbour entrance. It was *HMS Polygon* which had sped up and down the line of ships, maintaining a lookout for any U-boats. Luckily, none appeared the while. So now it was time for her to dock too, and unload the few wounded men that she had on board. On the entire journey back, stoker Jones, who also doubled as the medic, had worked tirelessly on patching up Lieutenant Bartlett; he had managed to plug up all the wounds and stop any more blood from escaping from his body, but had no idea if Bartlett was bleeding internally, just wished and prayed that he had done enough to save this hero's life. Bartlett of course had always planned to die. He wanted to die, he expected to die, and when he finally fell into the sea, having taken yet one more bullet, he knew he had died.

For him everything was black, and that is exactly how he wanted it.

"Jones, how is our man coping?" enquired Lieutenant Commander Harris.

"I think I have stemmed the bleeding, but I wouldn't like to say if he will live or die: the Lieutenant is in an awful way, with many wounds. My guess is that he will be lucky to see this day out, but we all know how amazing the human survival instinct can be. But we must land him first."

"Have a look in his breast pockets and see if you can find out who he is." Jones fumbled about and pulled out Bartlett's pay book. He glanced at it, then looked up at Harris, and added:

"It seems his name is Lieutenant David Bartlett, sir."

"Bartlett! That name seems familiar to me. Where have I heard that previously?"

But before he could think about it more, a real doctor came on board, looked at Bartlett, and had his men whisk him away to hospital.

Harris shrugged, and then continued worrying about the rest of the wounded and his crew, whom he owed a good breakfast to, except that now it was going to be a dinner, plus a few pints of beer; they had earned it, and he was going to make sure that they received all that they deserved.

"Men! Attention! When all the work is done on this vessel which has served us so well, I want to take all of you for a meal and some beer to say thank you on behalf of the Admiral. If he knew what we were going to do, he would want to join us."

There came a few whistles and "Oh yeah?" But generally the response was good. He saw that his brother's vessel was also tied up, and went over to see him.

"Where is Lieutenant Commander Harris?" he enquired to the first rating on the craft. But before he could get an answer, a head popped up from the engine room, covered in sweat and oil.

"Michael, how the heck are you?"

"I am glad to see that you are alright as well. Did you see much fighting? Did you rescue anyone? We had a dinger of a journey, saved a real bally hero who was called… er, oh crickey; I seem to hold nothing in the old coconut these days. It will come to me. Anyway, this Lieutenant saved so many men and really distinguished himself, quite amazing. Listen, Andrew, I am going to take my men for a meal and some beers, they have worked like demons, and I am so proud of them. What about you coming along with us?"

"Nice one, Michael; I should do the same, but they have already disappeared, or at least most of them have. They will be down the mess or the local pub, and quite honestly, good luck to them! Where shall we meet, and when?"

"Let's say at six o'clock tonight at the dock gates, number one?"

"Fine, how many of your men are coming too?"

"Well, it would have been nice to have had all fifteen, but I guess that one or two will want to do their own thing, and I will have to post a couple of men on the boat. I would guess about eight."

"What about telephoning that chap, what's his name? You know, the friend of dad's; he is stuck here, he might enjoy a rowdy evening with Jolly Jack Tar?"

"God! I had forgotten all about dad dying. I feel terrible now, but with all that's gone on… Good idea, he might like being cheered up. You can do the honours, you telephone and get him to meet us at Gate one at, what time did I say? Oh, yes, six o'clock. See you then, bye."

Dock activity had been frantic since their return to Dover. All the craft that had safely come back had been re-armed, re-fuelled, and made ready to go straight out again, if the need arose. Any damage that had befallen an unlucky vessel was already being put to rights. *HMS Vindictive* was already having her torn and bent superstructure pulled away, and ship repairers were going over her with a fine tooth comb; nothing would be overlooked and once started, they would carry on through a twenty-four-hour, seven-day-week work schedule until the jobs were done. The two ferries, *Daffodil* and *Iris*, were also docked and being re-booted for when the Admiralty could return them in pristine condition to their owners. Dover dockyard was a buzz of busy people, all getting on with the various tasks that were allocated to them.

In the meantime, Admiral Keyes had reported to the War Cabinet and the Admiralty that to his knowledge the whole mission had been a rip-roaring success, and he was already pressing for various medals to be presented to this sailor or that Marine, to this officer or that rating or Private. VCs were definitely going to be part of the rewards, or his name wasn't Roger!

Six o'clock came and Michael had the company of six of his men; the others were either married and wanted nothing more than to see loved ones again, or they had duties to attend to. But to Michael, six was a good number. There at the dock gate was Andrew, plus Inspector Cutler and a Constable whom he didn't remember the name of.

Andrew introduced them again to Michael.

"This is Inspector Cutler with Constable Williams, you remember, the friend of dad?"

"Nice to see you again, Inspector; even if it was only the other day, it has been a lifetime for us."

They all made their way to the '*Green Dragon*', which also served very good food, and plenty of it. The tables were taken according to rank: one for Michael's men and the other for Andrew, himself and the two policemen. After all, treating your men is one thing, but it would not be right to sit and converse with them as well: the Navy frowned upon that sort of fraternisation.

"So, Michael and Andrew, I am sure you have both made your mother proud; I know your father was terribly proud of you both and never stopped talking about what you both got up to. So what you *are* allowed to tell me, do!"

"Well, John, may I call you John?" asked Michael, speaking first.

"Of course you can, that is my name."

"Well, John, these last twenty-four hours have been momentous: Andrew and I had never been so close to the action before, and I know we have both done our duty. We even saved some real heroes; we saw things that one would only read about in boys' magazines. For the life of me, I have to stop and let the whole episode sink gently into some sort of organised framework, or everything will be just a blur."

Andrew chirped in with his ha'penny.

"The guns became so hot, some of our machine guns just jammed until we threw water on to cool them down. But our craft sustained no damage whatsoever, which I am very glad about. It was Michael who saved the real hero though, and once we have reported who he is, I am quite sure he will be due for some sort of medal, which in Michael's opinion should be the highest."

John chewed at his lamb cutlet, looked at Williams who was struggling, trying hard to cut a potato which was insisting on rolling around his plate, and then asked:

"Who was this hero, and what did he do to deserve so many accolades from you two?"

Andrew looked at Michael who glanced back at him blankly, scratched his chin thoughtfully and then said:

"He is a Royal Marine Lieutenant, but for the life of me I just cannot remember his name, though I did ask our medic to read it from his pay book. It will come to me sooner or later. But the fellow was a real hero of the first order: he saved the lives of three of his comrades, even to the extent of nearly losing his own. It was as if he wanted to be shot, and he did manage to be hit by maybe six to eight shots or shrapnel in various places. Men like him you only read about, never seeing them for yourself, so to be entirely honest I feel humbled at being there, and grateful that it was my craft that actually fished him out of the drink."

At this point a waiter with a long white cloth wrapped around his middle came over and asked for any more drink orders, then checked if it was alright to ask the men on the next table if they would like more beer. The answer came that anything the men wanted was fine, but woe betide anyone who got drunk and disorderly. Andrew and Michael ordered large rums for themselves and two pints of ale for the two policemen. All duly came, and just as quickly got drunk. The evening was turning out to be a great success, as all were having a fine old time of it.

They laughed and joked, and gradually nerves came back to normal and brains were being wound down, as everyone became relaxed and comfortable.

Some of the men started a singsong, and soon the entire pub was swinging to '*All the nice girls love a sailor*' and '*The Rose of no-man's-land*', '*It's a long way to Tipperary*', and many, many more. All too soon the bell was rung for last orders; Michael paid the bill in full, and told his men that they could have the rest of the night off, but to be ready and back at work at eleven o'clock the following morning. Just before Michael and Andrew went their ways, they asked John Cutler about their father.

"Was it this case that killed him? Is the man you were after still alive, or is he dead? Have things progressed any further, since the other day? Do you know when the funeral will be and where?"

"Whoa, one at a time, please!" laughed Inspector Cutler. "Firstly, I am not sure why your father died when he did, but I do know that the case was a huge burden for him to carry. He was desperately trying to nail the killer before he struck again, and believe me, they always strike again; these men are psychopaths of the worst order: they have very little feeling for anyone, or too much, depending on each individual. But they are always a danger and must be taken out of service, tried, then hung for what they have done. As I told you last time we met, I could not get to our man as he was commanding a unit on your raid, so I have no idea whether he is alive or dead; if he is alive, I shall get him, no matter what; if he is dead, then justice is done, even if it is not seen to be done. At least the streets will be safe from this butcher. And your last question is also hard to answer; I rather think you should telephone your mother and ask her when and where the funeral will be." He then added: "His body was sent back to his station at Plymouth; I guess he will be taken from there to a chapel of rest awaiting burial, which will be entirely up to your mother."

"You are a good man, Inspector; I know you have done your best, and had there been anything else you could have done to save him, you would have done it."

Then Michael turned to Andrew and said. "Andrew, it is time we went back to the docks. It has been a fine night, and I for one, have now calmed down enough to sleep easily in my bed, and that is exactly what I want to do, right now."

The four men walked out into the darkness. It was a fine clear night and Andrew looked up at the stars, and then watched as a shooting star flashed briefly by.

"Well, John, I hope you catch your man. It has been really nice getting to know you and Constable Williams, so thank you for coming. Do let us know how you get on, catch the bastard!"

"We will. Tonight has been a real pleasure; I wish we could have got to know you both with your father being here too. But, there you go. Stay healthy, don't let the Hun too close to these shores: we live in a beautiful country, and we have a wonderful language; it would be sad to have to start speaking German!"

They all laughed and shook hands. Cutler and Williams turned to walk towards the Castle, while Andrew and Michael made for the docks. Michael had only walked about ten paces when he stopped, turned on his heels, then called after Inspector Cutler.

"I have just remembered that hero's name: one Lieutenant Bartlett, I think. Goodnight!"

Cutler stopped dead in his tracks, pulled a tired Williams around, and shouted back: "*Who?*"

XII

All the wounded had been immediately transferred to various hospitals around the town of Dover; for some inexplicable reason, Lieutenant David Bartlett was sent directly to the makeshift hospital within the Castle enclosure. Maybe it was that he was an officer, or a member of the Royal Marines, or that his fellow Marines had asked for that transfer so that they could all come and support him, as he battled to recover... He lay in a bed within a small ward with five fellow Marine officers, all badly wounded, but none quite as seriously as Bartlett. His wounds had been well dressed and he did not seem to be bleeding internally, as colour was starting to come back to his face. Doctors looked in very regularly, but there was no change: he was in a deep coma, one that Major Carson, the chief doctor of the little hospital, thought he would never recover from. But his men thought otherwise. At every hour of the day a member of his unit would be sitting by the side of his bed, waiting for any signs of improvement. The first twelve hours after being taken in the hospital were the most critical, but none of his men would flinch from being there by his side.

"Sergeant Laker, is there any real point in men almost standing guard over the poor wretch?"

"Major Carson, sir, this man saved many men on the mole; it cannot be wrong to be with him and try and will him to live. He is a bloody hero, sir, someone who cares for other people; his men love him and so do I; so if there is no medical reason why we shouldn't stay, please allow us that right."

"Well, when you put it like that, what can I say? But don't touch; you could in fact make yourselves useful while you are there: get your men to offer their services to the nurses. They can empty chamber pots, and wash floors and generally make themselves available, agreed?"

"I will convey your wishes, sir; someone will be here by his bed twenty-four hours a day, he deserves that!"

"From what I have heard about this remarkable young officer, he will be in line for at least a medal. Right, duty calls; I must get on: the sick don't seem to want to mend themselves; I have to do everything for them." Then Major Carson laughed with a squeaky little woman-like cackle, and walked away, leaving Sergeant Laker wondering just who needed that particular doctor?

"Yes, that's right: Chief Constable Jolly! Tell him it is urgent."

Cutler looked at Williams, winked and smiled at the same time.

"Sir, is that you? Yes, it is a bad line; it always seems to be a bad line from here. Sir, we have him! He was brought ashore yesterday and is in the castle hospital; at the moment he's in a coma, but we have him, and that is all that matters. It seems our man has excelled himself and proven to be a blasted hero by saving the lives of some of his own unit. He has been shot maybe a dozen times or anyway quite a few. They are not sure whether he will indeed recover, but I won't let him die; he is due to receive more than a bloody medal: he will be awarded the honour of the hangman's noose, or my name is not John Cutler."

He once again winked at Williams; today Cutler was feeling on top of the world. He knew there was no mistaking this man, he was the killer. When the fleet had been at sea, he had very carefully searched through all of Bartlett's belongings. And there, in one corner of his personal chest, were three small trophies which linked him to the three girls: two were signed watercolours, the last was a silk scarf with the initials of 'CR' on them, and the label confirmed that the scarf had been bought in Plymouth. Cutler knew that he had enough circumstantial evidence alone to convict

Bartlett, even if he couldn't produce a signed confession.

"Anyway, sir, if it's alright with you, Williams and I will still hang on here until we can bring him back. He seems to have a lot of powerful friends; we don't want to lose him, do we?"

"No, John, we don't, but make it quick. Barbara Harris has been to see me and wants to talk about a funeral date; I want you to be there to give a eulogy on behalf of the force. Harris was a good man, and I want him to receive the best sendoff possible. The force has agreed to pay for the funeral, and it has also been accepted that the grieving widow will receive a full pension."

"Great news, sir, I worried about that. She would soon fall into difficulties without that pension. Anyway, sir, if there is nothing else, I would like to go and visit our man, see how he is."

Cutler asked to see Colonel Chartiers, and was shown into a private office, one he had not been to before. After what seemed to be an eternity, but only around fifteen minutes later, Chartiers breezed in, and silently sat down. He had a deep frown on his forehead.

"Inspector Cutler," he said with a rather awkward tone of voice that immediately worried John, "we have a major problem concerning Lieutenant Bartlett. I am quite sure you know what you are doing, but the blasted fool has made himself into a real life hero. His men worship him, and that worries me no end. I have never seen an officer so close to the enlisted men before, it is positively frowned upon. There are classes to consider, not to mention the discipline factor. But they love him, and the fool took it upon himself to save some of his own men, plus he seems to have fought the enemy and killed many. I keep hearing the word '*Bally Hero*' bandied about like a refrain. Anyway, Admiral Keyes, who knows nothing about the, er... er... crimes you talk about, wants to present Bartlett with a VC. Can you believe that? One of my men, and a possible killer to make things worse, winning the VC? Anyway, you can obviously see my dilemma."

"Well, actually no, Colonel, I cannot. It is beyond doubt that Lieutenant David Bartlett, one of your own officers, is a three times killer of young lovely women. Now, I don't care how loved he is by his men or Admiral Keyes, or the King himself, that man will hang!" With that last word he brought his fist down hard on the table. "Sir, I will not allow this man to get away with these crimes; where is your sense of justice, what the heck are we fighting this stupid war for, if it isn't justice?" He was bright red in the face, and puffing wildly, so much so that Constable Williams gently placed a calming hand upon his shoulder; this immediately brought him back down to earth, but with a bump.

"Well, of course you know your own business, but be warned: these men are not easily taken off track once they have set their wheels in motion. I cannot stop you seeing him, but do be careful, and don't talk about him to anyone; very few know the truth at this time, let us keep it that way, please!"

Cutler and Williams left the office and walked towards the hospital quarters, Cutler still fuming.

"That bloody cretin! How dare he suggest that we think of forgetting about Bartlett's little misdemeanours, as if he had just crossed the road at the wrong place? Why, the man is a serial killer of the worst order! I could bloody well scream! I feel so used and walked upon. Well, I am not going to be put off by any small-minded Colonel."

"Well, to be perfectly correct, Inspector, the Colonel didn't say you should let him go, just tread carefully; that is really what it was about."

"Not you too? Give me strength, Williams! Couldn't you see what the man was driving at? He may not have said it, but by God, that is exactly what he meant!"

They both entered the small building which temporarily passed as a hospital. Major Carson was there to greet them both as they entered.

"I have been expecting you two. Come to see the star performer, eh?" He scratched his nose, looked at his fingers then added quite softly:

"Better be careful what you say, Inspector, the man is in a coma; I don't think there is much chance for him, but his men are willing him to survive; they have set up a vigil by his bedside, and I don't like that, but they made sure I came off this one second best. He is a special man, that is for sure. I know why you are here, and he must suffer for what he has done, but I wouldn't be in your shoes for anything at this time, so watch what you say. If asked, you are just admiring a hero."

Cutler and Williams went over to the bed that Bartlett occupied. One Private Skoudie jumped to attention before he realised that these were two civilians.

"Come to see a hero, sir?"

"Well, yes, we have come to see Lieutenant Bartlett; I keep hearing what a wonderful man he is. Is he really that good, Private?"

"He is better, sir. He always puts his men first; why, in training, he works us hard, but always does more than we do himself, if you get my meaning? When anything has happened to a member of his unit, he is the first on the scene; he will always be at a bedside for anyone, always with a cheery word. When we were training on bloody barges, one man fell in the drink; the Lieutenant didn't hesitate: he was in there dragging the man to safety. Can't do enough for us he can't, so we are here for him now."

Cutler smiled at Skoudie, then looked close into the face of Bartlett; there, was his trim moustache, and above his left eye, one scar.

'I am in no rush; you just get better: you and I have some talking to do!'

Cutler turned to Williams, nodded, then they both left. Skoudie sat down once again next to his charge.

Four days of complete frustration went by. Cutler and Williams took in all the sights and even went to the theatre to see a terrible variety show that bored them both stiff. They met up with Andrew Harris one more time, but heard that Michael was now on patrol. By meeting up with Andrew, Cutler had gleamed some information concerning their father; this would be used in the eulogy that he had to give at the funeral. They walked along the shoreline, but that was quite difficult as they got challenged every other hundred yards or so; they therefore decided to do some hiking inland instead. However Kent hedgerows made it difficult to see anything on a walk. They did not like to use the car for their pleasure: apart from their concern for the lack of fuel, as it was a police car it only brought attention to themselves, and all they wanted to do was pass time until Bartlett roused from his coma. On the fifth day, word was sent that Bartlett had stirred several times, but was still in a deep sleep. Once again they appeared at his bedside; this time they were not going to leave until he awoke. Corporal Murrey was on vigil at the bedside when they appeared, and no amount of badgering could get him to leave. A small moan came from Bartlett; he turned his head for a brief second then was quiet again. A nurse appeared and quickly turned him onto his other side, explaining that if she didn't he would get terrible bedsores. Two more hours went by, then Bartlett made some eye movement and licked his lips which were always being kept wet by his men. An eye opened briefly; there was absolutely no sign of alertness, but he was obviously close to coming round. The doctor was called over; he scrutinised Bartlett's face intently, then bent close to his ear and started saying,

"Time to wake up, Lieutenant, time to wake up."

Some mumbling sound came from his throat followed by a movement with his head again. An arm jerked, but this was obviously painful because he winced at the effort. The young doctor gently patted his cheeks, then tried a little harder,

"Come on, Lieutenant, the day is late, time to get up!"

Both eyes opened; this time there *was* some life in them. He was awake. The doctor spoke to Bartlett quietly, just loud enough for him to hear, but not that loud that all could hear.

"There are two policemen here; they will not leave until you speak to them. Time to wake up and do what must be done."

Lieutenant David Bartlett spoke for the first time since the raid, his voice a mere rasp.

"Am I dead? Is this purgatory, heaven or hell; where am I?"

"No, none of those places," said the doctor with a smirk, "you are in the castle hospital at Dover. You have been on a raid and been severely wounded; this is the first time you have spoken since you went into a coma."

"But I wanted to die, I expected to die; why am I here?"

"You were rescued when you fell into the sea off Zeebrugge mole. You have been hit with bullets and shrapnel four times, and are lucky to be alive. Do you feel strong enough to talk to the two policemen that are here?"

"Well, if I am alive, then it is right that I speak to them, but can I have a glass of water first?"

Corporal Murrey was very reluctant to leave the side of his officer; that was until the young doctor threatened him with telling the Colonel and bringing a charge of insubordination against him.

Cutler moved in closer to Bartlett, put his head down to near the Lieutenant's, close enough to be heard and close enough to hear what any answer would be.

"You know why we are here, don't you, Lieutenant?"

"Yes, I know. What now?"

"You will be formally charged with the murder of three women. One young lady from Plymouth, one from Edinburgh and one from Harwich. You will then be taken back to Plymouth where you will stand trial."

"What will happen to me?"

"Bartlett, I am quite sure you will hang."

"If I tell you about others, will you let me die quietly here in my hospital bed?"

"I am in no position to offer you any deals. It would be good for your immortal soul should you tell me the complete truth, but it will not save your life, not for one minute. And anyway, you are now on the mend, you will live, not die."

"Look, I love my men, and I love the army. I really am not bothered what people think of me outside of these barracks; but I want to die with some sort of dignity, surely that is not too much to ask?"

"Tell that to the three women you killed, what dignity did you give them? Are there really any more unsolved murders that you have committed?"

"Yes, er... what do I call you?"

"Inspector Cutler will do. Now tell me about the others."

"I killed my sister when I was about seven years old, or eight, I forget. I pushed her into the sea at Eastbourne, off the pier. I hated women, I have never quite understood why, and you are not going to get some psychiatrist here to analyse me now. I really don't care any more for the why or how, I just did it and that is that." He turned his nose up, and flinched badly, as at this time he was experiencing extreme pain from his wounds.

"If you promise to leave me alone for half an hour, and that's all I ask - in case you're worried you can position someone by my bedside - I will then tell you where you can find the answers that you seek." He waited for a reply, but none was forthcoming. "If I don't tell you what I know, you will never find out the whole truth."

"Why do you want to be left alone?"

"I am dying; nothing you can do will change that. My destiny was to be on that raid and it has been fulfilled; the plan was to die at Zeebrugge, but some well-meaning fool saved me. I know I was a hero, I knew I would be, that was what I was born to do, and it has been achieved; there is no reason to stay alive, and I am not going to. Do you want that information or not?"

"Yes I do; I will do anything to clear up your appalling actions from the past. You know, Bartlett, some murders are almost forgivable, but the way you slaughtered these girls was completely beyond the pale. And now you say that there were more, it is hard for anyone to feel any pity for your predicament. Basically, what you want is to be left, with your colleagues thinking of you as a bally hero, right?"

"Make up your mind, Inspector; I *am* going to die, nothing you say or do will alter that fact, and I am *not* going to the gallows: I will be dead in the next thirty minutes." Once again, he winced in pain.

Cutler looked at Williams as if searching for support, but nothing was forthcoming.

"What I will do, if what you say is true, is that I will not allow the newspapers to get hold of your name. Your parents will never know what a demon they spawned. First though, I really want to know why you hated these women so badly."

"I really am not that sure anymore; I hated my sister because she was older and bullied me all the time. My mother, now dead, was an old lady when I was a toddler and I always felt that she turned a blind eye to my sister's incessant bullying, just like all women whose weakness is that they shrink away from unpleasantness. As for my father, he merely followed my mother's lead since she was the dominant one in the marriage, after my sister that is. I am not sure why I hated women, and I hope you noted the word *hated* not hate. It has all lapsed since Zeebrugge, like I said; after that nothing really matters any more. I guess, to give you some sort of answer, women always annoyed me; they were always there, too close, yet you could never rely on them, always letting you down in some way or another. The world seemed a nicer place without them, and when a woman came close to me, I really couldn't stand it, and that was what happened with the three women you are investigating: they wanted me, and I didn't want to be wanted. They were clever and bright, too bright for their own good. They all had to go; I had to show them that I was brighter, cleverer, and much, much stronger. One thing, Inspector, they all died quickly; they must have felt nothing, it was so quick." Bartlett had turned quite white but still managed to smile as he remembered all the past events.

"Give me the names of the others."

"No, I won't give you the names, because I cannot remember them, some go back many years. But I will tell you where to go to get your information. Do I have your word that you will leave me for half an hour?"

"Yes, alright; it runs against the grain, but needs must and all that."

"I own a little cottage just outside of Hastings in Sussex; it is a little bungalow called '*The Retreat*', and it is up an unmade road called Mill Lane; there, in a drawer next to the fireplace in the dining room, you will find a diary, plus coded information concerning where you will find the remains of women that have met their maker through me. Now, I don't expect any respect from your quarter, but I want the men I loved to think well of me. Knowing you will keep your word, I will now want to have my last minutes alone."

"What do you mean your last minutes, how do you know you will be dead soon?"

"Because since we have been talking I have spent that time opening all my wounds. I didn't have much blood left when they rescued me, I really cannot have much left now!"

It was then that Cutler noticed a small but growing pool of blood spreading under the bed.

"Oh, shit, the bastard has already tricked us! Williams, fetch a doctor, quick!"

But Lieutenant David Bartlett was now drifting off into a dream state again.

Williams rushed out of the ward in search of a doctor. Cutler, bending down again towards Bartlett, asked:

"What was so special about Zeebrugge?"

"Well, it just turned out to be quite a pleasant little journey, and it has left me happy, and surely, Inspector, happiness is what we all crave for in life, but for me it is in death. You will never understand, never!"

Cutler had to stand helplessly by the bed for quite a few minutes, impotently watching Bartlett gradually slip away before Williams and the doctor came running back into the ward. The doctor felt for a pulse, opened an eye, looked closely, and then, emotionlessly, pronounced him dead.

The Inspector looked at Constable Williams, and then declared as they started for the door:

"I never did understand what he was talking about, except at the end when he told me I would never understand". Cutler chuckled softly to himself, in a knowing way. "Well, that part was probably right, anyway." He sniffed and chuckled again. "Let's make our way to Hastings; our work is not done yet."

On seeing that the two policemen were making themselves ready to leave Dover Castle, probably for the last time, Colonel Chartiers called them into his office.

"I cannot say it has been a pleasure, gentlemen, but I will say that you have both been professional in your handling of this delicate situation. But, and there is always a but, I have had Downing Street on to me concerning our mutual newly departed friend, Lieutenant Bartlett: you must sign the official secrets act. I am sorry but you will never be allowed to talk about this business. I am to warn you that if ever anything concerning Bartlett comes to light, you will both be prosecuted. And you will go to prison, that comes from the top. Sorry, but it seems we need a hero more than we need the truth. Lieutenant David Bartlett stays the hero he always wanted to be. I have it from a higher authority that he is to be awarded a posthumous VC. It is good for his family, but most of all the country gets a '*Boys Own*' real life story to wonder over. Is that entirely understood? If so, please sign here, and I do mean both of you."

They signed, got their passes, and then drove out of the castle's main entrance. "For crikey's sake, Inspector," said Williams as they passed the portals for the last time, "if I ever see Dover again, it will be too soon!"

Remains of the destroyed bridge which ran over the canal at first lock, Zeebrugge.

View of the destroyed pier at Zeebrugge. "Thetis" is visible centred above in this shot.

British convoys and mine sweepers used in the raid.

A different perspective of "Intrepid" and "Iphigenir" blocking the canal at Zeebrugge.

Captain Fryatt (left) who captained the SS "Brussels" (right) which sank during its charge at the Mole.

Memorial of the "Vindictive" Heroes, April 23rd 1918.

They shall grow not old, as we that are left grow old:
Age shall not weary them, nor the years condemn.
At the going down of the sun and in the morning
We will remember them.

For The Fallen (1914), Laurence Binyon.
(Segment of Poem)

Epilogue

The raid on Zeebrugge and Ostend took place one minute after midnight on the 23rd April 1918. Seventy-five ships were sent on the raid, along with three block ships whose sole purpose was to obstruct both canal entrances. In Zeebrugge the British did manage to get several hundred Marines landed onto the mole, a concrete and granite structure which stretched one and a half miles into the North Sea. The attacking forces were expecting light defences, but things never turn out as one expects. Both Ostend and Zeebrugge were being defended by massed armed forces with large contingents of artillery, both on the mole and on the shoreline. In the attack on the mole two hundred Marines and sailors died, four hundred more went into captivity. As Admiral Keyes saw the three block ships enter the harbour area, he assumed, wrongly, that the battle had been a complete success for the British. But the truth is that the only real success came from the two ageing submarines, *C-1* and *C-3*, which managed to ram themselves under the viaduct, and then blow up, destroying the structure; this stopped reinforcements from making counterattacks against the Marines left alive on the mole. Sadly, all three of the block ships were hit so many times by gunfire that none could position themselves in such a way as to be really effective in stopping the U-boats from moving either in or out of the canal: the U-boats could still squeeze past and enter either the canal and the comparative safety of Brugge, or go back out into the North Sea and attack British shipping yet again.

What Keyes thought was a wonderful success, in the true British naval tradition, was in fact an abject failure. *HMS Vindictive* which played a pivotal role in the raid did make it back to Britain, only to try again some weeks later, this time to be sunk off the mole. But the press and Admiralty never stopped saying that Britain had won a major victory at Zeebrugge, instead of admitting the fact that it had been an unmitigated disaster, and this disaster at Zeebrugge was echoed at Ostend with no gains at all.

Why was this raid a miserable failure? Mainly because, like most plans in the Great War, it was badly thought out with too many clues allowed to get into enemy hands. It was once quoted that what was agreed in the morning at the war cabinet was read over dinner by the Kaiser. Regarding plan ZO, as it was called, the Kaiser did in fact know all the details. Some weeks before, a small flotilla of ships had done a practice dummy raid on Zeebrugge; it had gone badly wrong and one of the coastal motor boats managed to get itself stuck upon a mud bank just outside the harbour. The Germans caught the small craft, and resting on the Commander's portable table was the Admiralty's complete plan for the actual raid. That certainly turned into a pleasant little journey!

But the Admiralty need not have worried. The Americans were now joining the Allies on the Western Front and the U-boat scourge was being addressed by better equipped surface vessels that now found it easier to blow a submarine out of the water.

On the 11th hour of the 11th day of the 11th month, Germany signed the armistice treaty. World War One came to an end and the world was at peace... at least for the time being.